WHEN WE ENTERED THAT HOUSE

CLAIRE L. SMITH

ISBN-13: 979-8-9933182-0-2

Also by Claire L. Smith

Helena

Agnes and Cat

Contents

For all the queer kids from small towns

Part One

IN 2003, I TURNED ELEVEN. I think we'd just gotten the internet in our house but our TV was still the size of a cardboard box. Years have passed since then, yet the same anxiety and chest-heaving terror haunts me as if I were still a child. That's the issue with children; they may not remember every word you said or exactly what you did, but they will always remember how you made them feel. Yet, people wonder why I don't want to have children of my own.

School had just ended, but I wasn't going home. I could never admit to myself why I never wanted to go back. I guess I was still convinced that my parents screaming at each other for hours on end was normal. *Everyone's Mummy and Daddy love each other like that.*

Usually, I'd walk home with Elle Harris. She was in my class and we both liked storybooks and sitting at the back of the classroom, so we were best friends. When adults looked at us, they'd always coo at how 'different' we were. Elle had dark hair that reached her armpits, a slim build with agile legs that could carry her for miles. She also had dark freckles across her nose and full brown eyes that always seemed to tremble in their sockets.

She wore large jumpers with holes at the cuffs, second-hand trainers that were too big and jeans that, to this day, make me wonder whether they were the same jeans as the previous day or several different pairs bought in bulk.

At the time, I was blonde with a short, blunt bob that my mother had picked out at the hairdresser's. Over my moss-green eyes, I wore wide-frame glasses to help with my inherited blindness, and I'd always be clothed in a light sundress and stockings that would rip and tear on the playground or in the woods.

That's where we'd go. Every afternoon, we'd take the 'long way' back. Instead of cutting directly through town, past the locally-owned shops, the market and the run-down movie theatre, we'd head to the outskirts towards Mortimer Hill. We'd follow the road away from the school, turning left until we reached the rims of the towering trees that stood as tall as the skyscrapers we'd seen in picture books. Neither of us had ever left the tiny village, so the idea of a building over three stories high excited us.

We followed the skimming road, aiming for the forest path up ahead that would lead us down into the realm we'd escape into every day. The forest felt like our own little slice of calm, an isolation in which we wouldn't be bothered by the concerns of the outside world, with no adults around to ruin our time.

That day was no different; we went along the trail as carefree as two outcasts could be, pointing out long-legged bugs and strange, twisting vines.

Our brisk walk was suddenly interrupted by a faint whirring that broke though the peaceful silence. I ignored it, thinking it was simply the breeze caressing the leaves of the trees until a hard force slapped me on the back. I let out a choppy scream. I stumbled forward, red residue flying over my shoulder as the paint-filled balloon burst against my spine. I froze, shocked, my glasses falling forward against my nose.

"Jessica, no!" Elle screamed.

Glancing over my shoulder, I saw three figures riding bikes, their shoulders hunched over the handlebars as they carried several more paint bombs in their front baskets. My eyes narrowed towards the most familiar face in the centre of the trio. Jessica was maybe fourteen at that time with long brown hair tangled into a messy braid, arched eyebrows, freckles and a pair of dark eyes that fixated on us like a hunter's gaze. Her lips were angled into a wet grin as her two friends cackled on their bikes behind her.

"I got the princess's dolly dress!" she cackled, reaching forward to pick up another bomb.

I felt a firm hand grip mine before I was yanked into the forest, following Elle as the blunt splats of the paint bombs hunted us. We sprinted through the trees, my eyes fixated ahead as my fear forced me forwards. My dainty buckle shoes did little to help as Elle powered ahead, her scrawny arms pumping and her backpack jolting with every step.

The older girls' laughter began to fade as we disappeared into the forest. They parked their bikes as they watched us.

We'd normally follow the road for longer before dipping into the forest, so I wasn't completely familiar with my surroundings, an uneasiness sinking in like a winter chill. I tried to brush it off, glancing down at my now-ruined dress with a pouting huff.

"Your sister is so mean," I muttered.

"Sorry," Elle murmured.

Turning, I gawked at Elle as she stood before me, her lips tilted into a deep frown. Red paint splattered down the back of her large, algae-green jumper as if she'd been ambushed by gunfire. It trickled down the fabric and dribbled down the calves of her jeans.

"Mum will kill me," Elle said, clenching her soft jaw.

"The red matches your shoes," I replied, pointing my toe towards her reddish sneakers. "It'll be fine, you can tell her Jessica did it."

Looking back, I always scold myself for saying that. I was such a bubbly, pathetic little thing, so drunk on childhood naivety that I would push away any frightening mention of reality and retreat into my books. Now, I feel like my tongue is soaked in lemon juice, the things that I once loved sour against my gums.

Setting down my baby pink backpack, I pulled out the vibrant green library book before joining Elle on the forest floor, our legs folded and our eyes fixated on the pages. I can't remember the name of the book I'd checked out that day, but I remember it was about a trio of troll-slayers who'd sneak out in the middle of the night to fight the monsters that wanted to take their loving parents away. The illustration is fuzzy in my mind, but I remember the trolls were meant to be as tall as trees with long claw-like nails and teeth. It was one of Elle's favourites.

The forest had a strange relationship with time; the towering trees shielded us from any perception of it. I'd rarely hear any birds or animals, like they were afraid to sing. We'd remain there for hours, immersed in our created world until we'd glance up by accident to see the sky turning from the blazing pink of sunset to the bruised purple of night.

"Zoe," Elle said, "we should go."

I glanced up at the darkening sky, fear setting in with the early evening cold as my frightened child-mind latched onto every creeping shadow and misshapen tree branch. I stuffed the book back into my backpack before slinging it over my shoulder. I watched as Elle dusted the dirt from her pants, then looped her arms into her own brown backpack. There was a silence as both of us glanced around at the distorted forest floor. A lump lodged in my throat as each tree suddenly became reflections of the others, like we were trapped in a house of mirrors. The more we stood in silence, the longer the woods stretched out before us. It was slowly pulling us into its depths.

"Which way?" I asked, trying to hide the anxiety trembling in my chest.

Elle did not reply, her owl-like brown eyes scanning the forest as the hollow breath of wind passed through us. I dipped back into my childhood innocence, gripping Elle's hand before picking a spot in the growing darkness.

"This way," I said.

With every step, I kept pushing back any fear that welled within me, yet my knees began to tremble and my heart pounded against my ribs. *The path is just ahead*, I convinced myself, *it has to be*. The trees grew black as the sun sank into the horizon. The cold bit through our clothes until I finally stopped, my hot breath running up my throat. I gripped Elle's sweaty hand as we stood alone in the dark, the once peaceful serenity of the forest morphing into a dark sympathy of rustling leaves and crunching twigs.

Elle squeezed my hand as we glanced around the clearing in which we stood, trying desperately to pinpoint our path as light dissolved from the sky, leaving us under a veil of black. A cold sweat ran down my spine. I pressed my shoulder against Elle's arm, huddling us together as tears began to prick my eyes, my mind a buzzing hive of racing thoughts.

Then I saw it. My eyes ran up the base of Mortimer Hill, climbing higher until I saw the blurred outline of the house... *that fucking house*. It was as black as the sky behind it, making me question if it was there at all. But it was. Its presence clutched me, a tight grip around my throat. It seemed to blend into the ocean of trees that surrounded it like a concealing cloak, the dirt path leading towards it covered with seasons of dead autumn leaves and rough patches of grass. At the peak of the two-story house, a warm speck of light glowed from the center window. It was as small as a pin, yet its flickering warmth pierced through the shadow of the house. Through the lens of my glasses, I fixated on it, a strange numbness overcoming me, smothering any fear that pulsed through my body.

"Do people live there?" Elle asked.

I can't remember if I responded to her. I don't even remember sliding my foot towards the house. I just recall rushing backwards with Elle's hand latched onto my elbow, her widened eyes boring into me as my senses returned. I squinted in a blunt confusion, glancing around the clearing as if I'd just awoken from a deep sleep.

"If the big house is that way... then town is *that* way," Elle murmured, pointing a limp finger in the direction opposite the house.

"...yeah," I replied.

Once again, we dipped into the darkness with Elle ahead, her spine hunched as if waiting for a new monster to lunge out from the curtains of shadow that surrounded us. My fear formed a lump in my throat as I took in a trembling breath. My skin prickled and my chest twisted as we sprinted forward until at last, our feet met asphalt. A long breath eased from my burning lungs as I pressed my palms into my bent knees. The daunting forest walls scratched at my back as we followed the road, dipping further into the dimly-lit streets. We slowed to a numb walk, our hands still intertwined as we wandered the quiet streets. Despite the leftover fear that lodged in my chest, I felt a strange urge, an almost indescribable tug back towards the forest. Just as I tried to push away the urge, the light in the window of that house appeared before my eyes, as if it were calling me back.

When we reached my house, we paused at the front gate, almost unsure of what to do with ourselves. I could hear them inside, yelling at each other as usual. I still held Elle's hand. I didn't want to let go.

"I can get my Mum to take you home," I said.

Elle glanced towards my front door that kept back the muffled, aggressive voices from within.

"No, thanks," Elle replied, "I can walk."

"Can your Mum pick you up?" I asked.

Elle shook her head, reaching to grip the straps of her backpack. My stomach twisted as she turned from me. I didn't want to be alone with only my parents and my mind. Even from outside, I could feel their mutual venom spilling from their mouths and spreading throughout the house, ready to consume me the moment I stepped inside. I looked at Elle as she faced the darkened road, her form shrinking as the cold night gripped her. I didn't want her to be alone either.

"You can stay here," I said. "They'll be quiet eventually and we'll both fit on my bed."

"I can go by myself," she mumbled.

I glanced over Elle's shoulder into the night. The cloaking shadows and the long road sent a strong chill down my spine. Yet, glancing back at Elle, I couldn't let her go alone.

"You don't have to," I said, stepping towards her, "I can go with you."

"No, you'll get too scared," she replied, her voice dropping like a rough stone before a light sigh escaped her lips, "...see you tomorrow."

My face dropped, my shoulders hunching as I felt the hard punch of Elle's reply. *You'll get too scared*. I decided to believe that, my self-doubt taking over.

"Okay, sorry..." I replied.

I let the numbing night breeze sink in as Elle walked away. I watched her form get smaller and smaller until she resembled the tiny light from that house—until the darkness finally consumed her.

"Goodbye," I whispered to myself.

With heavy legs, I approached the front door. The yelling slapped me like a hot breath of air as I stepped inside. I hunched my back as I crept through the foyer. I peeked into the living room to see them, roaring and growling at each other like wild animals, their faces red with a boiling rage and their bulging eyes fixated on each other, and nothing else.

My father still had hair back then, grey tickling his dark locks—locks that fell over the rims of his thick glasses as he yelled, and veins running up his thick neck as if they were strangling him. Beneath lay a nest of shattered glass, a reddened cut oozing from his hand from when he must have smashed the flowerless vase that used to live on the coffee table. My mother had a nude-pink nail polish on. She jabbed her colourful fingers at my father as if her vile words weren't enough to throw. I could never decide which animal scared me more.

"I'm sorry I'm late," I mumbled, "I can do the dishes to make up for it."

A part of me wanted to raise my voice so they could hear me, but the last time I'd done that, they screamed at me for yelling before aiming their sharp words back at each other. So, I waited, hoping that my mother would see the dirt and grime on my clothes, or that maybe my father would glance at the clock and notice the hour. I just wanted them to see me.

My stomach twisted in my chest, and a sourness swelled in my throat before I turned towards the kitchen.

"I'm going to get some dinner," I said.

Their arguing followed me like a shadow; it hovered over me as I pulled a microwave meal from the freezer. I counted as I waited for dinner to heat up. I tried to focus on the numbers counting down instead of their yelling. I can't remember what they were fighting about—but then again, I don't think they remember, either. I used a clean tea towel to hold the microwave meal's hot plastic, the steam licking my face as I carried it towards the stairs and into my bedroom.

My mother would always show other adults around the house if it was their first time visiting, and my room was her second favorite next to the kitchen. I always had to stack my plush animals a certain way on the bed whenever I made it, making sure my pastel pink cover was free of creases before adjusting the white, sheer curtain that dangled above the head of the bed. I think the only thing I chose out of that room were the books on my princess-castle-shaped bookshelf.

Looking back, I feel a pang of guilt for being such a spoiled brat about that room, and for hating it whilst vaguely understanding that some had it worse than me. I placed my dinner on my mattress, taking a book from my shelf before sitting down to escape. I tried to block out the argument between taking mouthfuls of food and scanning the page.

The next morning, I sat in the back of my father's car. From the front seat, he sat like a statue, his posture as straight as a ruler and his eyes fixed on the road. He hadn't spoken to me all morning. I'd gotten myself up as usual, overhearing my mother purposefully bang and smash pots and pans together in the kitchen as she made breakfast. I had cereal, flinching every time she took her anger out on the poor stove or countertops. I'd collected my things, gotten myself dressed, then waited for him in the car. I told him "good morning," but he didn't reply.

We sat in silence as we took our usual route. A part of me wanted to ask him to put on the CD player or the radio to soften the silence, but I was too afraid to ask that much of him. I didn't used to be so tense around him. I have brief memories of him smiling at me, of trips to the park where he'd carry me home on his back and of the occasional bedtime story where I'd snuggle up next to him and encase myself in the warm, fireplace-like feeling that no one could hurt me. I still don't know when that ended, but he gradually began to withdraw, like winter sucking away the warm summer weather. I only ever saw him hunched over his desk in his office or snapping at people over the phone. I'd end up reading books in bed waiting for him to come join me, but he never did. As an adult, I could conjure up a few reasons why, in an attempt to ease the empty feeling he caused—but as a child, I couldn't wrap my head around it. All I knew for sure was that I was desperate to get him back.

Thinking back to earlier, I recalled seeing his navy-blue tie as he slipped into the car, my innocent mind sparking at the chance to make him smile.

"I like your tie, Dad," I said.

"Since when do you care about ties?" he replied.

My sudden smile faded, my spine sinking into the seat as I sealed my lips. I thought it was my fault—I was dressed in an outfit my mother chose, and I had her eyes, her nose and her blonde hair. I reminded him of her, and it was all my fault. We pulled up to school and the car came to a sudden halt. Grabbing my backpack, I slipped from the vehicle, glancing back at my father as he turned away.

"Bye, Dad," I said, "I love you."

He shifted his head slightly, almost as if to look back at me. I stared at the side of his cheek, the tips of eyelashes barely visible. He sighed before turning his head once again to stare forward. *That weak bastard*.

"Just stay out of trouble," he sighed.

I paused, as if waiting for more, my eyes falling with my hope.

"Okay," I replied.

I readjusted my backpack as I entered the schoolyard. The splashes of color coming from the playground equipment did little to liven up the otherwise grey buildings and asphalt. Aside from Elle, I had one other friend. Not a best friend, as the rules for eleven-years-old girls say that you can only have one. My other friend's name was Tina. I could never look her in the eye, but she rarely noticed. She had a nice laugh and always wore a pretty beaded necklace that her dad made for her at a Dad-and-Daughter event the school held once for Father's Day. My father couldn't come.

I found her sitting in her usual spot, in the second-to-last row of the class, directly in front of me. She waved, prompting my cheeks to burn.

"Hey Zoe, look!"

Tina pulled back her black hair to reveal a tiny star-shaped earring, the gold shining against her dark skin as she beamed at me.

"Mum finally let me pierce them!" she said.

I leaned in to get a better look, smiling at her before sliding into my seat. We talked as the rest of class began to settle in, my eyes constantly drawn towards the door until the bell eventually rang.

"They're so pretty," I replied. "Where's Elle?"

"I dunno," Tina replied. She turned around in her seat to check the door herself. "Maybe she's sick."

Resting back in my seat, I kicked my feet as I thought of Elle. *Why was she late? She made it home, right?* These thoughts filtered through my mind, feeding the twisting knot in my chest until that house we'd seen in the forest came to the forefront. I bit my lip as the image of it flashed before my eyes, my shoulders hunching as a sharp chill ran up my spine. Every time I'd see that house, normally by accident when Elle and I would wander too far into the woods, this feeling would overtake me like a winter flu. I wouldn't be able to remove it from my thoughts, its shadow haunting me like a clingy nightmare.

I was flung back to alertness as the classroom door clicked shut. Elle passed the line of desks, her face edged towards the floor and her hands clutching her backpack straps. I frowned when I noticed she was wearing the same green jumper as yesterday.

I glanced over to our teacher, Mrs. Holt, I think her name was. Mrs. Holt never said anything to Elle about being late that day, but her eyes followed Elle as she made her way to her chair. Her face was soft, as if she was staring at a sad puppy before she stood up to commence class.

Elle slipped in next to me, dropping her backpack by her seat before letting out a long sigh. I took in her appearance. Her hair was knotted and her eyes were bloodshot with bags gathering beneath, yet all I could notice was that the red paint on her jumper had been scrubbed away, leaving only slight patches of transparent paint.

"Your shirt looks better," I said.

"Yeah, Jess helped me," Elle replied.

"Why?" I asked, my face twisting in confusion.

"I don't know," she replied. "Do you have any snacks?"

I leaned down and dipped my hand into my bag, digging for my lunchbox and the chopped apple slices inside. My mother didn't like me sharing snacks with Elle, so I started telling her that I was just extra hungry, but then she worried about me 'getting fat' so I sometimes ended up sharing. I gave Elle two of the four apple slices, watching as she took a large bite, juice flying from the fruit.

I looked down to see Mrs. Holt's legs as she knelt down next to the shortened desk, leaning in to whisper something to Elle—something I couldn't hear. Elle nodded to her before slipping from her desk, grabbing her backpack before following Mrs. Holt from the classroom. I kept my eyes on the door as the class eased into a contained chaos at the absence of the teacher.

"Where are they going?" Tina asked. "Is she in trouble?"

I shrugged.

"Mrs. Holt didn't look mad," I replied.

Tina quickly moved onto another topic, but I kept my vision on the door until Mrs. Holt returned without Elle. Turning back to Tina, I watched out of the corner of my eye as the teacher crossed the classroom. I analyzed her demeanor. She wasn't stomping her feet like my father, she wasn't huffing like my mother—no clenched fists or bitter muttering—no puffed chest or cold shoulder. The knot in my chest eased slightly as she squatted down by the space between Tina and me.

"Zoe, can we talk in the hallway for a minute?" Mrs. Holt asked with a soft smile.

I shot a glance at Tina before slipping from my seat. I followed Mrs. Holt with my face aimed at the floor and my teeth lightly sinking into my bottom lip. Mrs. Holt closed the door behind us, enclosing the classroom noise inside before turning to me.

"Zoe," she said, "do you know what happened to Elle's jumper?"

My face fixated on the floor as Mrs. Holt hovered over me, waiting for my answer. My child's mind convinced me that I was in trouble, a fact that not even Mrs. Holt's warm voice and calm face could tell me otherwise.

"Jess threw paint at us... but she helped Elle clean it up afterwards," I replied, my chest tightening with every word.

"Oh, I see," Mrs. Holt said, pausing before she asked, "so did that happen on your way home?"

A thought poked through my buzzing anxiety, drawing me away from it like a moth to light. If I was in trouble, then Mrs. Holt would have to tell my parents. She'd maybe even call them in for a meeting where they'd have to leave work and their arguing and focus would be on yelling at me instead. The thought was both frightening and alluring.

"No," I replied.

"Where were you?" she asked, her eyebrows dipping slightly.

"The forest. I didn't tell my Mum or Dad."

Mrs. Holt's calm demeanour trembled at that, a sternness overtaking her eyes before the gentleness returned with her soft hand on my shoulder.

"Zoe, you always need to tell your parents where you are," she said. "They'd be so worried about you."

I frowned, blinking up at Mrs. Holt as she returned to her questioning.

"What time did you get home?"

"Um... I can't remember," I said, "but it was late and dark."

"What about Elle? When did she go home last night?"

"I don't know."

I kept my eyes on the floor, unable to lift them to meet Mrs. Holt as I gave a light shrug. She pushed again, rephrasing the question only to be met with the same response. I wasn't talking anymore. There was a stale silence between us before she let out a short breath, the smile returning to her face as her hand left my arm.

"Thank you for giving Elle your apple slices. You're a good girl," she said.

Her words slapped me harder than an open palm. My bushy eyebrows connected in the centre of my forehead as Mrs. Holt stood, reaching for the classroom door.

"Go on," she said, "I'll be back in a minute. We'll be doing some worksheets when I get back."

I gawked up at her, hesitating before returning to the classroom. Tina had started talking to one of the other girls so I sat in silence once I returned to my desk, sitting with an almost blank mind as I blended into the noise of the classroom.

I really shouldn't have been so hard on myself, especially since I was so young, but I couldn't help it. I think of that little girl sitting in the back of class by herself because she was too shy to talk to any other kids, unable to understand the adults around her, whilst trapped in a cloud of childish anxiety that would very soon be her pathetic downfall.

Elle came back several minutes later. Her hair was smoothed, and in her hand, she held what looked like the last few bites of a sandwich. I'm glad I didn't say anything about it when she sat back down. I asked instead if she wanted to go troll hunting again that afternoon.

I can only recall being inside Elle's childhood home about five times. Even so, I spent four out of those five times in the kitchen by the front door. I stood waiting as Elle disappeared upstairs to change out of her green jumper. By the stairs was the door to what I assumed was the living room. From the thin gap between the door and its frame, I could see into the darkened room. There was a cut-out of the flickering television, the rest cut off by the edge of a couch, a single arm slung over its side like a limp snake. By the size of his hand and growl of his snoring, I guessed it was Elle's father. I had no idea what his face looked like, but I knew his snoring and I knew what kind of beer he liked due to the pile of bottles that grew by the couch like festering weeds.

I glanced over the kitchen once more. I pressed my back against the counter and ran my eyes over the food-smeared countertops along with the various food packets and other everyday kitchen mess. A flashing fright shot through my body as the front door opened behind me, allowing Jess to storm inside.

"What are you doing here?" she spat, wide eyes centred towards me.

"Elle is getting a new jumper," I squeaked.

Jess's eyes stretched further as she glanced across the messy kitchen, tossing her heavy backpack on the floor before rolling up her sleeves and stomping towards the sink.

"Oh shit," Jess hissed. She glanced between the messy kitchen and the man in the living room. "What time is it?"

I froze before fumbling with my sleeve, pulling it up to reveal my watch.

"Four-fifteen," I replied.

Jess ducked to retrieve a sponge and cleaning spray from beneath the sink, placing both on the counter before she darted around the kitchen. She gathered the various food wrappers and packets before tossing them into the bin. Finally, she paused as she noticed the half-open living-room door.

"Is he asleep?" she asked.

"I think so," I replied.

She nodded to herself before reaching to close the door fully, huffing under her breath.

"Bastard can't even throw his shit in the bin."

Jess then turned to face the kitchen. She gripped the spray and sponge before getting to work on the countertops. I stood frozen in place, watching her through the curtain of my blonde hair. She swiped at the surfaces as if she were brawling with them. She paused once she reached a dried stain, her knuckles growing pale as she scrubbed at it. She muttered to herself under her breath, as if her thoughts were so frantic they couldn't be contained inside her head.

"Her next shift is at six, she'll be back by five. Hopefully, he's still asleep so he doesn't piss her off. I can have dinner ready by..."

Her murmurs died down, leaving only the gravelly squeak of her cleaning. The silence only tightened the knot in my chest as I took a short step towards the counter.

"Um, do you want some help?" I asked.

Jess didn't reply and left me to the stew in the silence for a moment longer. I tried a different tactic.

"Chores are the worst, aren't they?" I said with a hopeful smile and forced chuckle.

Jess stopped scrubbing, her grip on the sponge still tight. She glanced up from the kitchen counter, glaring at me through the thin curtains of her brown hair. A lump formed in my throat as I froze in place, the tension oozing off of Jess like an icy breeze.

"Yeah, sure, Princess," she huffed, shaking her head before turning back to scrubbing.

My face dropped, my eyebrows squeezing together as I clenched my tiny hands.

"I'm not a princess," I said, scrunching my nose.

Jess lifted her eyes again, her brow raised as she glanced up and down at my white stockings and pink plaid dress. She laughed in light amusement before a coldness consumed her face, her stone-like eyes falling back on me.

"You know, most little girls would die to have clothes like that," she said.

"You can have them then!" I spat. "Will that make you happy for once?"

Reaching up into my hair, I unsnapped the white hair clip that kept my fringe in place, my locks falling in front as I slammed it on the kitchen counter. Jess flinched. Her hands left the sponge as she jolted back in surprise. She stared at me as if, for once, I had properly left her speechless. I thought I'd feel powerful, maybe even triumphant, but I didn't. I felt as if I'd ripped off a piece of my skin to let her see the pain inside. I backed away from her with a rushing vulnerability.

The staircase creaked as Elle descended the stairs, wearing a deep blue hoodie and jeans. She looped her backpack over her shoulder before turning to Jess.

"I'm going to play," she said.

Jess turned towards her sister, her eyes falling closed before she released a long sigh, resuming cleaning whilst keeping her vision on the counter.

"Just make sure you're back before dark. I don't want to spend all night looking for you again. I'll make dinner for Mum, and I'll leave some in the fridge for you," she said. Her voice was gruff, yet a slight gentleness could be heard.

"Okay, thank you," Elle replied.

I wouldn't realize it until a few years later, but there was something in the air as we left that house. Something left untouched—unsaid—a thorn stuck deeply in both Jess's and Elle's sides.

Laying on our backs, the sticks and leaves crunched beneath our spines. We waited for our hot, panting breath to slow before drifting into a peaceful silence. The woods around us murmured with whistling birds and swaying tree branches. As my mind wandered, my thoughts landed back on Jess and the hair clip that remained on her kitchen counter. I teased the thought before rolling my head towards Elle, my peachy cheek brushing against the forest floor.

"Does Jess always clean like that?" I asked.

"Yeah, all the time," Elle replied, still facing the sky, "even when I try to clean something, she has to do it... but she's a little happier for a bit afterwards."

"Does she like cooking, too?" I asked.

"No," Elle said, shaking her head. "She doesn't know how to make much, mostly just mac and cheese, and toasted sandwiches."

"Maybe I could teach her how to make eggs," I replied.

"Scrambled?" Elle asked.

"No, just fried." I adjusted my glasses as I glanced back toward the pale blue sky, the tree branches reaching out across the clearing as if trying to smother the colour. "Why is she... like that?"

"Like what?" Elle asked.

"I dunno, sometimes nice, sometimes a...bitch."

Elle turned her head to frown at me. "You never say that word."

I shrugged, lifting my legs off the ground slightly to dangle them mid-air.

"It can't be that bad. Dad says it all the time," I replied.

"Don't let your Mum hear or she'll throw a tantrum," Elle replied.

I scoffed in mild amusement at the thought of my mother stomping her feet on the ground like a spoiled toddler, the image fading as I gazed up into the blankness of the sky. I let out a strained sigh before I kicked my legs again, catching sight of it from the curve of my shoe. From my position, I could only see the peaks of the rooftops rising above the curtained trees. My legs drifted back to the ground and my torso lifted as I kept my eyes on the house, my head tilting as I fell into its gaze once more.

I flinched as a breathy sound whispered in my ear, my hand reaching for Elle's.

"Do you hear that?" I asked.

It was faint and could almost be mistaken for a shaky breeze. Yet, it carried a shot of emotion with it like a strong river, the striking sorrow filling our ears and sinking into us. Yet, it was so soft, almost alluring, like a siren's call beckoning us to drown.

"Is someone crying?" Elle asked.

Part Two

AS WE NEARED THE HOUSE, I felt as if I were approaching a sleeping bull. With every step towards it, my stomach twisted tighter and tighter, and my mind dipped further into a numbed haze. An apparent dread slid up my body as we reached the front gate that had long since collapsed. Its black iron poles lay like skeletons in the dirt. The crying continued to call us until the soft whimpers turned into the long sighs of a siren call.

An alluring smell stroked my nostrils, like burned caramel—sickly sweet but acrid all the same. I stepped into the front yard, loosely dragging Elle beside me. The front yard was empty except for the few ashen remains of some long-dead shrubbery and rose bushes. The house itself looked like an old insect shell with most of its foundations bent or rotting away. The windows were shattered with the brown remains of the curtains lapping at the open frames. The black roof tiles littered the ground by the walls, abandoned where they'd fallen. I stared up at the house and watched the blackened walls stretch up towards the clouds. My eyes landed on the single window from where the flickering light had called for me the night before.

We followed a cobblestone pathway that was invaded by moss and erosion. It led to the short veranda steps and front door that nearly tore me from my trance. Unlike the rest of the house, the double front doors stood perfectly upright despite their lack of support, the wood smooth and glistening against the soft afternoon sun. They were painted a deep crimson that glowed against the sunshine, the doorknobs polished and glistening orbs of gold.

I wouldn't let go of Elle's hand as we wandered further up the cobblestone path, climbing the veranda steps until we reached the double doors. Readjusting my grip on Elle's palm, I listened again for the soft weeping, noticing that it seemed to vibrate from the door.

"Do you think they're lost?" I asked. "Or scared?"

"Or lonely," Elle said.

I glanced down at the doorknobs, hovering my hand beneath the one closest to me, watching as golden rays of light clung to my skin.

"Maybe we should go back," Elle said. "I'm hungry... and Jess said I should go back for dinner."

I still can't describe the feeling that engulfed me. The soft crying poisoned my mind, pulling me into a state of delirium. I wanted, more than anything, to open that door.

"I want to go in," I replied.

Elle didn't respond, keeping a passive grip on my hand as I latched my fingers around the doorknob. The metal's coolness sent a gentle electricity buzzing through my joints. Elle paused before she reached out herself, clasping the other doorknob before we both pushed forward.

Light spilled into the deserted foyer; our shadows spread across the weak wooden floors. Stepping inside, we found the tongue of a winding staircase leading to the upper floors, and two open doorways on either side of the room. The doorway to our left led to a large yet empty room, whilst the one on the right revealed a room with a dust-ridden fireplace. I felt my nose tickle due to the filthy surroundings, dust clinging to air particles around us.

"Who would want to hide in here?" I asked, scrunching my face in discomfort.

A loud bang echoed from behind us, causing a sharp scream to run up my throat. My hand latched onto Elle's arm as we spun around to find the doors now firmly shut. My heart pulsed in my chest, burning as I glanced at Elle, who stood frozen in my grasp, her hands locked by her sides, her rabbit-eyes wide.

"Elle?" I whispered.

Elle blinked and let out a shaky breath as she glanced around the room, her eyes sharpening once again as her jaw eased open. I followed her gaze, my eyebrows shooting upwards in a slapping shock. The dust and empty rooms were gone, revealing crimson-coloured walls and polished wooden floors. The staircase had transformed into a mahogany masterpiece with swirling patterns carved into the fencing and a lush rug tumbling down the steps. A gasp of shock lodged in my throat as I looked through the two doorways, watching as the left transformed into a spacious living room with a grand piano, red lounges and armchairs, and flickering oil lamps.

"Zoe?" Elle said. "The crying... it stopped."

I broke from my stunned state to listen for the weeping. The air was still and the chatter of the forest disappeared, leaving nothing but a dead silence. I scanned the foyer as I turned my ears for the noise. I squinted until I spotted the room on the right. Inside lay a large dining table with eight matching chairs that were taller than me. On its surface was a large feast filled with bread rolls, roasted vegetables, several salads and trays of sides with a plump pig laid out in the center, a gold-painted apple shoved into its mouth. I wandered into the room with an open jaw and Elle on my heels, her own watering mouth open.

With a slight grin, I opened my nostrils, the smell forcing its way up my nose like a hard punch. My mouth watered as the smells soaked my nose and tongue. It smelled better than my grandmother's kitchen or the local bakery, so hypnotising in its alluring scent. Yet, beneath the bubbling euphoria lay a trembling caution—a small voice that whispered a firm hesitance, a voice I happily ignored.

As I gawked at the table, Elle reached down and extended her index finger to lightly poke a platter of fruit. She blinked as her skin pressed against one of the sugar-dusted cherries, her face creasing in confusion.

"If you're hungry, maybe having one would be okay," I said.

"Are we allowed?" she asked.

I gave a light shrug, reaching to pinch the side of the tray. Like Elle, I was hungry after having to share my lunch and snacks with her. I shook off my temptation and began to retract my hand. That feeling clasped me once again, holding me in place with my fingers mere centimeters from the fruit. It came with a voice, chilling and icy like a snowflake slipping into my ear.

"Eat...enjoy..." it whispered.

I didn't hesitate. I did what I was told.

I reached down and plucked a sugar-coated cherry from its pile.

"Zoe?" Elle protested.

I ignored her, shoving the cherry past my lips and sinking my teeth into its fragile flesh. My senses rushed back to me, keeping the cherry between my teeth as I absorbed what I had done. There was a stone-like silence before I glanced at Elle.

"What does it taste like?" she asked.

Curious myself, I began to chew. My teeth teased the hard pit as the fruit juices spilled across my tongue. Yet, even as my teeth bit into the pit of the cherry, I could not taste a thing—the fruit was devoid of flavour.

"I don't know," I replied. "You try."

Elle hesitated, like I had, but finally reached for her own cherry. She frowned as she popped it into her mouth, her cheek expanding as she chewed. My eyes flashed as a sudden taste smacked my tongue, a metallic flavour filling my mouth. I froze as the cherry fell back into my throat, my chest heaving as I began to cough, covering my mouth as the half-eaten cherry and its hard pit tumbled down my oesophagus. Then came the burning sensation. It filled my mouth as if I'd just gargled stinging nettles. I glanced at Elle as she, too, began to cough, her eyes watering as she bent over with her hands on her throat. I groaned between coughs, my eyes landing back on the table to find a large jug. I reached for it, grasping it in both hands to carry its weight. I glanced down into the liquid within the jug before lifting it to my lips. It tasted like the cherry had tasted—metallic and chemical—yet it soothed my burning tongue. After a long gasp, I handed the jug to Elle who grappled it after taking a long gulp, lifting the jug until she drank her fill.

My body shivered as I absorbed the liquid's taste, my chest contracting as I examined my now-wet hands. I assumed it was water due to its transparency, yet the lingering flavour continued to stain my mouth.

"What was that?" I asked between shallow breaths.

Elle glanced into the now empty jug before setting it beside the cherries. She wiped the forced tears from her eyes.

"Blood..." she said. "They both tasted like blood to me."

My mind drew a blank, my stomach clenching at the horrid thought. I cleared my throat before searching the room for a distraction, evading the thought of how Elle could know what blood tasted like. Past the dining table, I noticed the black curtains that now covered each window. The fabric was thick enough to block any evidence of sunlight. Rounding the table, I approached and pinched the fabric before attempting to draw it back. To my surprise, the curtain barely budged, as if it were pressed into the wall. Frowning, I gave it another hard tug, the tough fabric slipping from my grip as it remained flush against the window.

I glanced back at Elle, only to find her staring off towards the other end of the room. On top of the lit, polished fireplace hung a large portrait that took up the majority of the wall behind it. I followed Elle as she approached the painting. She tilted her head as she examined it. The portrait contrasted with the remainder of the room. The frame was brittle and rotting, the canvas swollen and blue. The figures—two women and two men—were disfigured by the peeling layer of paint, except for one. There was a young girl in the corner of the portrait, her long black hair curled into ringlets. The girl's eyes were warm brown, and freckles covered her nose. She wore a navy-blue dress with a matching glove that held the hand of the boy who stood next to her. The boy's face, like the two adults in the portrait, was smudged and erased.

"She's really pretty," I said.

Elle's eyebrows dipped as she took another step towards the portrait, reaching to place her fingers on top of the mantlepiece, her brown eyes gazing up at the girl.

"She looks sad," Elle replied.

I glanced back up to the portrait, my perception twisting as I zoned in on the girl's face. Her eyebrows were slightly dented, her lips tilted upward, eyes empty.

I squeaked as a sudden chord breathed through the house, slapping our backs as we turned back towards the foyer.

Another followed it, morphing into a melody. The piano's tune continued as I glanced at Elle, her face sunken in confusion. Approaching the entranceway, we stuck close to the stairwell to avoid being seen. With light footsteps, we eased towards the doorway to the living room. Pressing the small of my back against the wall, I bent forward slightly with Elle hovering behind me. I caught a glimpse of the piano, yet the stool was empty, although pushed out from underneath. Maybe the player was standing. I took a half-step towards the doorway, my jaw going slack as no one stood by the instrument, not even a shadow. The melody continued for a few more notes before it suddenly halted, dipping us into silence once again.

Elle and I slipped into the room. My eyes darted from one wall to the other before landing back on the piano. I stepped towards it and pressed down on one of the keys. No sound came from it, only a slight tap from the pressure of my finger. I tried again, tapping keys at random, but still no sound came.

"Is someone making fun of us?" I asked, suddenly angry.

I glanced back at Elle, who gave a light shrug before a slight sniffle eased through the room, the crying resuming in the absence of the piano. I flinched, my ears following the weeping up the winding staircase in the foyer, whimpers bouncing off each step. Elle stepped towards the staircase, lifting her foot to press her paint-covered trainers against the first step, gradually adding her weight. The staircase did not creak or whine under Elle's foot. It only echoed with the crying from above.

We climbed the staircase to the second story and found a dim, candle-lit hallway full of doors. The crying lost its direction, filling the room as we wandered past the several doors that lined the dark, wooden walls.

"Um... hello?" I called.

The weeping did not falter.

"I'll try in here," Elle said.

Elle reached for one of the doors and pulled it open before poking her head through. I held my breath as she lingered in the doorway, a pulsing anxiety flaring within my chest at the idea of separating. The urge to cling to her only increased as Elle disappeared behind the door, leaving me alone in the hall. I pushed away my fear. If Elle could go off on her own, so could I, right?

I glanced around the hallway, looking for a door to choose. I paused as my eyes landed on the door at the end of the hallway. It was much taller and thinner than the others with a slight golden tinge to the paint. My posture bent as I stared at it, an unnerving sensation crawling up my body as it towered over me. I tried the door next to it instead.

Inside the room stood a large four-poster bed with deep red curtains hanging from its tall posts and matching bedsheets and pillows. There was a dressing table opposite the door with a large mirror and several assorted items laid neatly on the surface of the table. I stepped forward to examine them: a hairbrush, hairpins and what I assumed was makeup, although I noted it wasn't the same as the kind my own mother used.

I bent down to check under the dressing table and found it empty. I kept my crooked posture as I turned to check under the bed, finding only a few stray dust bunnies. I sighed before rising to my feet, my heart leaping into my throat as I peered past the curtains surrounding the bed. There was a large lump in the center of the mattress, reaching from the pillows to the opposite end of the bed. The red comforter covered it completely, as if someone were hiding beneath it. Yet it was perfectly still, unmoving like a statue. I gawked down at it, as if waiting for it to stir or scream at me for waking it, if it was sleeping at all.

Holding my breath, I took another step towards the bed, my eyes unblinking as I gawked at the lump. I reached for the blanket and pinched the cover before pulling it back. With my breath still captive in my chest, I found a deep dent within the mattress. It mirrored the odd shape of the comforter, matching its curves yet there was nothing to fill the seemingly empty space.

"Hey Zoe?"

I flinched before turning to see Elle standing in the doorway, her eyes scanning the room before landing on me.

"What's this room for?" she asked.

I paused in thought.

"I think it's the mum's bedroom," I replied.

"...but wouldn't the dad sleep here too?" Elle asked. "The other bedroom had a shaving kit and everything so..."

I felt my muscles tense. I knew the reason why Mummies and Daddies stopped sharing bedrooms, I just didn't want to admit it to myself, even after my own parents hadn't shared a bed in months.

"Maybe the dad snores," I said, more like a deflection than a reasoning.

Elle shrugged before slipping back into the corridor. I turned back to the bed, and the deep crevasse within the mattress. I tilted my head before lifting my arm towards the dent. I paused as a sudden cold engulfed my fingers, crawling up my palm before disappearing as I retracted my hand. I hunched my shoulders as I peered down at the bed, knitting my brow before extending my hand once more. I teased the intensity of the cold, pulling away my fingers once more before I gradually inched them closer and closer to the mattress.

"Hey Zoe, look at this!"

I paused, my hand hovering over the dent. I gave a light shrug before stepping away, the cold touch lingering on my fingers. I followed Elle's voice down the corridor to the front of the house. I glanced once more at the towering door at the end of the hall before slipping into the room to its right. My eyebrows shot up to my hairline, my glasses slipping down my nose as I took in the room. The walls were covered in a pastel yellow wallpaper with picture frames of cross-stitched lambs, rabbits and swallows peppered across its surface. There was a large but short bed in the center of the room with duckling-yellow sheets and several purple and pink pillows piled on top.

I took another step into the room, glancing behind me to find a large wardrobe wedged in the corner by the door. Next to it, under a single curtained window, sat a desk-sized dollhouse. It was painted a dusty red with pink windows and a beige roof. In front of it sat several dolls. They sat with their soft backs against the doll house, their sewn-on smiles beaming up at us.

"Hey, this one is pretty," I said.

My excitement blinded me as I bent down to pick one up. It had bright yellow curls and an orange dress.

"Zoe, maybe we shouldn't—" Elle said, pausing as her eyes widened, "... the crying's stopped."

The silence settled in like a thick fog. Deep confusion sank in and my body flinched as a light tap landed between my feet. Glancing down, a wave of relief washed over me as I noticed that the doll's wooden shoe had slipped from its fabric foot.

"Oops," I said, bending down to pick up the shoe.

I pressed my knee against the floor, steadying myself as I placed the shoe back on the doll's foot. As I lifted my gaze, I peered under the bed, my muscles tightening like a hangman's knot as I spotted a pair of feet dangling off the other side. I froze in shock before lifting myself up to my full height. On the opposite edge of the bed, facing away from us, sat a girl in a white gown, her black hair tumbling down her back. I tightened my grip on the doll, glancing toward Elle as colour drained from her face, her eyes fixated on the girl as we waited in the icy silence.

"Why are you in my room?"

My hand lashed out to grip Elle's. The girl's voice was soft yet harsh, like a snake's hiss. I shifted backwards, slipping my shoulder behind Elle's as her jaw trembled, her piercing eyes blinking as she searched for a response.

"W-we heard you crying," Elle stuttered, "we were worried."

The girl remained unmoved, leaving a pause before asking, "Why did you touch my doll?"

My heart clenched in my chest.

"Um, I-I'm sorry," I replied, glancing back to the dollhouse, "I'll put her back."

"Wait."

I froze in place, glancing back towards the bed as the girl slipped from the mattress, my shoulders hunching as the bed released a low creak. My eyes fixated on her as she rounded the bed, the veil of her black hair covering her face as she turned to face us. Terror cut through me as I saw her face, the face that would haunt me for years to come. She had pepper-like freckles across her thin nose, long eyelashes and eyes as blue as a summer sky with slightly clouded pupils. On the front of her dress was a bright yellow bow that matched her hard dress shoes. Yet, her skin was a transparent pale, the iris of her eyes was a light grey instead of black, her joints looked swollen against her twig-like limbs, and across her face lay a long, red scar reaching from the corner of her left eyebrow to the curve of her chin. She looked so sickly in comparison to the bright yellow of the walls that surrounded us. She was like a wilting lily amongst a field of sunflowers.

"Do you play with dolls too?" she asked.

Her facial features were so stiff that she could only manage to slightly lift her eyebrows in a sickly hope. Elle didn't respond, still squeezing the blood from my hand with her vice-like grip. The girl continued to stare at us, her lips perking with a dreamy smile.

"I have more," she said.

She walked as if she were floating, with no echoing footsteps following her as she reached for the cupboard by the door. She opened the wardrobe doors to present us with her offering. Inside were several short shelves, each with at least five different dolls, all of them sitting in neat rows. Some had smiles sewn onto their faces, some slight frowns or gaping grins. Each one also had their own outfit and unique expression, as if every one of them had a distinct personality and backstory.

"These are my friends," the girl said, lifting her finger to the first doll on the top shelf, "this is Lydia. She lives in the village with her mother, and this one is Jean, she works on a nearby farm with her brother; she loves the cows there."

She kept going, working down through every doll. I glanced at Elle from the corner of my eye, sharing our mutual confusion. There was something about the girl's voice that still sends shivers down my spine. It was squeaky and bright, yet breathy and stretched. It was painfully obvious how much she wanted to impress us, and it only made me want to leave, but a swelling fear—and a layer of pity—kept me in place.

"What about this one?" Elle asked, extending her finger towards another doll.

The girl's face lit up, her bony fingers flying to the doll in question, holding it up to Elle.

"This is Julie," the girl said.

"I-I like her dress," I mumbled, glancing past Elle to look at the doll's salmon pink dress.

"It's like yours," the girl said.

Her eyes landed on me again. Her proximity gave me a closer look. Her greyish pupils almost matched the bright blue of her eyes, like a cloud against a clear sky. Yet, they set off a slight twist in my chest, as if I were staring down a dark alley. At the same time, I couldn't look away from her spiderweb gaze.

"Yeah," I replied, my voice thin in my daze.

She beamed at me before her eyes fell to the dollhouse, placing the Julie doll next to it before reaching to unlatch its front. She pulled it back to reveal the house's interior. It almost resembled the house in which we stood, with a large living room, dining room and kitchen with four bedrooms upstairs. I took a step forward to admire the detail in the palm-sized pieces of furniture, my eyebrows rising in astonishment. The girl scurried back to the wardrobe, gathering an armful of dolls before placing them next to the Julie doll.

"Come on," she said, sinking to her knees in front of the dollhouse.

I glanced at Elle since I wasn't sure of what to think. She opened her mouth as if to object but gave in and joined the girl on the floor. I hadn't played with dolls in a little while since both Elle and I were starting to grow out of it, but we went along with what she wanted, mostly because we didn't know what else to do.

Internally, I tried to guess her age. She was just as tall as I was so I assumed she was also eleven but the way she spoke and the child-like daze in her eyes made me think younger, plus her sickly appearance smothered any other indicators. As she played, she would occasionally hum under her breath. The tune was strange but soft, filling me with a slight calmness as we continued to play.

"So, you live here?" Elle asked.

"Yes, my father owns the whole estate, the village and everything," the girl replied.

Frowning, I glanced at Elle, who met me with the same sort of stunned look. Yet, she prolonged it, lifting her eyes to the window. *I want to go home,* she mouthed. I gave her a light nod before turning to the girl.

"Um, do you maybe want to go outside?" I asked, "It's nice weather outside."

The girl paused, her eyes lifting towards the window. She stared at it as if she were gazing up at a monster, her eyes quickly falling back down to the dolls.

"I don't like going outside," she replied, her voice firm.

"That's okay," I replied, bowing my head before turning back to the dollhouse.

From the strained silence came another melody, the piano music travelling up the staircase to meet us. I frowned, unsure of whether or not I was imagining it, until Elle glanced at the open door.

"What's that?" I asked.

"Oh, that's just my brother. He practices a lot," the girl replied, voice bittersweet. "Do you have any brothers?"

We shook our heads.

"You're lucky," the girl replied.

Her face soured for a moment, as if an ugly thought passed through her. I glanced at Elle, clearing my throat in discomfort.

"Um, I have a sister," Elle said.

The girl's face lit up again, her cloudy eyes widening slightly as she aimed them at Elle.

"I always wanted a sister," the girl said. "What is she like? Does she play with you all the time? Do you spend all day together?"

Elle gawked back at the girl as if caught in a pair of blinding headlights. Her jaw fluttered for a few seconds before she could mutter out a soft, "No..."

The girl's excitement faded. She glanced off at the corner of the room.

"Oh, I thought that's what sisters did," she mumbled, "I'd hoped that's what sisters did."

"What's your name?" Elle asked.

The girl looked up from the dollhouse, tilting her head as if she'd almost forgotten, her eyes sparking as it finally came to her.

"Eva," she said, "what's yours?"

"Elle."

"I'm Zoe."

Eva smiled, the scar on her cheek bending to her rising lips.

"Um, thank you for letting us play," Elle said. "But, we need to go now."

Eva blinked at us, her face dropping into a light, dreamy frown.

"Why?" she asked.

Elle hunched her shoulders, shifting closer towards me as Eva kept her hard stare locked on her. "M-my sister needs me," she said.

Eva's eyes landed on me, as my mind raced for an excuse. My first thought was to mention that my parents would want me home for dinner. Yet the response died in my throat as the question popped up in my mind. Would they even notice if I never came back?

"My, um... I have school tomorrow," I replied.

Eva let us stew in a tense silence.

"Elle, which one do you like the most?" she asked, her voice light as a feather as she pointed at the dolls.

I watched as Elle scanned the dolls, her eyes landing on one with a green dress, brown hair and freckles drawn onto its white-fabric skin.

"That one," she said, pointing towards it, "green is my favourite color."

Eva leaned forward to pick up the doll, shifting against the floor so she properly faced Elle, holding the doll out to her with both hands.

"You can take her with you, only if you promise to bring her back to play," Eva said.

Elle glanced away from Eva towards me. I gave a small shrug before she turned back to Eva.

"Um, okay, I promise," she replied, taking the doll. "See you soon."

Eva didn't say another word as we rose from the floor, her eyes set on where we'd sat beside her.

"Um, bye," I murmured.

Yet she didn't move, her eyes unblinking as she stared at the floor.

"Goodbye...I'll be waiting," she said.

A chill ran down my body as she said that, her voice burning into my brain. We hurried to the stairs. My hand locked with Elle's as she gripped onto the doll. The piano continued to play as we reached the first floor. I was tempted to check the living room again, but as if sensing our approach, the music stopped as we neared the exit.

As I reached for the front door, a sudden hold gripped onto me. A strange doubt told me to go back upstairs and play some more. I pushed it to the back of my mind, giving my head a light shake as I gripped the door handle. Confusion struck me as the door jarred in my grip, refusing to open despite my desperate tugging.

"Is it locked?" Elle asked.

I grunted, pressing my body into the door before it finally buckled against my weight. I let out a satisfied sigh before stepping outside. I froze as I reached the porch, where a black sky full of blinking stars greeted me instead of a midday sun.

"How long were we in there?" I asked.

"Only a few minutes... right?" Elle replied, hugging the doll to her chest.

I readjusted my grip on Elle's hand before leading the way down the porch steps, the cold night air pressing against us as we approached the large iron gates. The temptation, the pull, to turn around grew stronger with every step. My pace slowed slightly before the gates finally loomed over me. I yelped as Elle pulled me forward through the gates. I didn't even realise I'd stopped walking. The pull decreased suddenly, as if I'd shrugged my backpack off my shoulders.

I gave Elle's hand another squeeze as we dipped into the forest, our shoulders brushing against one another as we tried to shield each other from the chill and the shadows that leered over us.

"That was weird. She was weird," I said, processing my thoughts by saying them out loud.

"Yeah... maybe just a little shy," Elle replied.

"It's nice that she gave you her doll," I replied, giving an indifferent shrug.

"Zoe?" she asked, "why did you want to go inside so bad?"

The question struck me like a bad hand. I still have no idea of any logical 'why.' I try not to think about it, even now.

"I don't know..." I replied. "Why'd you ask?"

Elle hugged the doll closer to her chest, parting her lips as she searched for a response.

"You seemed like you really wanted to. When you went to open the door...you were smiling, like really smiling," she said. "It scared me."

I remember the events of that night all too well. It happened so quickly, but it plays like a slow-motion action scene in my mind. When I arrived home, for once, it was quiet. I stepped into the living room, then the kitchen and no one was there. I heard some rustling upstairs and began to climb the steps. Halfway up, my mother emerged from her bedroom, a large suitcase trailing behind her as her heels clacked against the floor.

"Mum?"

She had that face on again, as if she'd taken a vicious bite into a lemon. Her expression was firm, her eyes cold and unfeeling. I felt my stomach drop as she spotted me, letting the suitcase slap against each step as she began to descend towards me.

"Come on, we're going to your grandparents' house," she said matter-of-factly, as if she were telling me the weather forecast.

Confusion gripped me, as I blinked back the tears scratching the backs of my eyes. I still don't know if she even noticed my reaction, or if she just chose to ignore it.

"Unless you want to stay here," she said. "You can decide who you want to live with."

"W-where's Dad?" I asked.

"With his whore. Come on," she replied.

My thoughts spilled through my brain before I lunged up the stairs, dodging my mother before I sprinted down the upstairs hallway.

"Zoe!" she screamed.

I burst into my room, slamming the door behind me as if it would protect me from anything. I ran to my bookshelf and gathered armfuls of books as the door swung open behind me, my mother storming in. Like a frightened mouse, I jumped onto my bed and burrowed into the covers.

To my surprise, she didn't yell. Instead, I heard a trail of footsteps across my room, my mattress dipping as she sat beside me. I didn't bother hiding my sobs as I felt her large hand rest on the flat of my back. There was no warmth due to the thick cover that separated her skin from mine, but the mere contact pressed down my sobs, pulling me from the dark cloud of panic that consumed me.

"Zoe," she said, her voice soggy and trembling under the threat of tears. "I know it's hard, I know it's scary."

The following pause drew me from the covers, my eyes peeking out to the crumbling woman before me. She sat with a ruler-like spine. Her form shook as if a slight gust of wind would send her tumbling. Her cheeks shone with tears and her eyes were red and puffy, yet she refused to look at me, staring at the door instead. I watched as she sucked back a sob, my muscles tensing as I soaked up the emotions that spilled from her eyes.

"But can you please just be good?" she asked, sucking on her lips, "for me?"

The urge to dive back into the sheets and shut her out overwhelmed me, my fingers gripping the bed cover as my eyes burned with tears. Yet, I wanted my mum. I crawled onto her lap like a sleepy cat, burying my face into the fabric of her pants as she wrapped her arms around me. Amongst my pulsing thoughts came a slight sliver of clarity, my body numbing as if I'd taken a vial of poison. My muscles softened as she ran a hand through my hair, but I felt so cold, like an empty vessel floating through a flowing river, having no control over where I went.

"Come on, sweetheart," she said, clearing her throat, "I'll get grandma to make you dinner."

My mother shrugged me off, standing before extending her hand towards me. I stared at her clammy palm, wiping my eyes with my forearm before biting back a leftover sob. Cementing my final choice, I took my mother's hand as I climbed from my bed, leaving the books where they had fallen. I kept my head down as we made our way back downstairs, collecting the suitcase as we went. The silence continued as I slipped into the backseat of my mother's car, leaving room for the rumbling of the engine and the gaping space between us.

Part Three

I **HADN'T SEEN MY GRANDPARENTS** since Easter because they lived two towns over, yet I wasn't as excited to see them as I thought I should've been. It was a Saturday but I spent every moment of it in the spare room I shared with my mother, only forcing myself out for breakfast, lunch and dinner. When my grandfather popped his head in at around eleven o'clock to ask if I wanted to play a game of snakes and ladders, I said no. At three, my grandmother asked if I wanted to make sugar cookies with blue icing—my favourite. I passed. It was nice of them to try.

They were relieved when I asked to see Elle, watching with a hopeful eagerness as I called her up on the landline.

"Yeah?" Jess snapped when she answered.

"Hi Jess, it's Zoe," I said, unable to spark even a polite positivity to my voice.

"You want to hang out with Elle?" Jess sighed.

"Yes, please."

There was static as Jess paused.

"Hey, what's the matter with you?" she asked. "You sound... pouty, Princess."

I didn't know how to reply. Even over the phone, there was a strange feel to Jess's voice, like she was actually somewhat concerned. I almost felt the urge to tell her, but the thought died upon creation.

"Can I just see her?" I asked.

"Okay, hold on," Jess replied, leaving me waiting for a few minutes before she spoke into the phone once again. "She says she'll meet you in the usual spot."

My grandmother dropped me off at the edge of the forest. She was happy that I had something to do, so she sent me off with a smile and a kiss on the cheek. I forced a smile before stepping out of the car.

"Tell Elle 'hello' for me," she said before gently easing her car down the road.

I followed the usual path to our favourite clearing. Elle sat propped against a large tree, her nose buried in a book and her green backpack resting beneath her bent knees. The late-morning sun hit her like a halo. She looked so at peace in her own little bubble.

"Hi," I said.

Elle glanced up from her book, keeping the majority of her face hidden behind the cover before dropping her eyes back down at the page.

"Hey," she replied. "Where were you on Friday? Sick?"

"Um, no," I mumbled. "I've been at my grandparents' since Thursday."

"Oh, are they sick or something?" she asked.

"No..."

I crossed the clearing to sit next to her, hugging my legs to my chest as I let the silence pass between us. Elle kept her book up, yet she didn't flip a page. I checked the cover. It was the one about troll hunters. It took me a while to build up the courage to speak, almost forcing the words from my throat.

"It's just that um, my, um, mum and dad aren't going to live in the same house anymore."

"Oh...?" Elle replied. "Did they say why?"

I thought back to the night we'd arrived at my grandparents. After dinner, I'd been told to go to bed but I spent most of the night overhearing my mother rant to my grandparents in the living room. She screamed for several hours before she broke down crying. When she eventually went to bed, she lay down next to me. I looked over towards her and didn't know what to think of her. A stranger might as well have crawled up next to me.

"I don't know," I replied, sinking against the tree trunk.

Silence consumed us once again. We used to sit there for hours just reading, but this time, there was something between us, like the real world had finally caught up to us. I glanced over to Elle who was still hiding behind her book, remaining still as if she was carved out of stone.

"Elle, what's wrong?" I asked.

Elle paused before she began to lower the book from her face. Shock rushed through me as I saw the purplish bruise blooming against her cheekbone. My lips hung open as Elle reached to unhook a lock of hair from behind her ear, easing it over half her face before she set the book down. I gave her time, waiting in eternal patience.

"I lost the doll," she mumbled. "Jess took it and I tried to get it back."

A strong sense of dread flushed through my body, my stomach dropping towards the ground.

"Jess did that to your face?" I asked.

Elle brought her legs to her chest, resting her mouth against her knees.

"No," she whispered, "we fought over it and woke up my Mum."

"I'm sorry," I said.

Elle didn't respond, reaching up to rake her fingers through her hair.

"What will Eva say?" she asked.

"She has a lot of dolls, maybe she won't mind."

"That's not the point," Elle murmured.

I shrunk at her hardened tone. Silence consumed us once again, the air around us thick with tension. With a long sigh, I tuned into the sounds of the forest, my eyes lifting to the trees above, watching as the clouds crawled across the blue sky.

I didn't notice the soft voice in my ear until Elle shuffled against the ground, tilting her head to also listen. This time, there was no crying, but a calming hum. My mind began to melt as the sound kissed my ear. Picking up my backpack, I climbed to my feet and waited for Elle to join me. We followed the song, climbing the hill before we found ourselves at the mouth of the iron gates once again.

The hold of the song faltered as we stepped into the front yard, a sudden awareness slapping us. I glanced at Elle whose dreamy expression faded, her shoulders hunching as a pale nervousness took over. I reached and gripped her hand, giving it a comforting squeeze. We climbed the crumbling porch and lingered in front of the door.

"We should probably knock this time," Elle said.

She lifted her fist and gave the door three hard knocks with her knuckles. As we waited, I glanced around at the rotting yard, my eyes lingering back over the iron gates. My muscles tensed as I saw a flicker of gold lunge out at me like a burst of sun. I squinted at the light as a faint figure emerged amongst the burst of gold. It was slightly taller than me with skinny arms and legs. A chill flushed through my blood as a slight, strained moan emerged from it, the desperation radiating from the cry before it and the figure burned out like a flame.

I turned back towards the door, trying to dismiss what I had seen as Elle knocked a second time. The door clicked, easing open to reveal the lavish foyer. Out of curiosity, I bent to my side to peer through one of the large cracks in the wall to find the empty ruins on the other side, straightening up to stare through the door again to see the foyer reappear.

I felt a chill run up my spine as the door closed behind us, my eyes landing on the piano in the living room. It was silent, but unlike last time, the stool was pushed out as if someone had, or was, sitting on it.

"Elle! Zoe!"

I followed the voice up the staircase to see Eva standing at its peak, grinning down at us. She'd added more ribbons to her curly hair and she'd added white stockings and shoes to match her yellow sundress. I felt underdressed in my flowy skirt and t-shirt.

"You came!" Eva squeaked, her cloudy eyes wide with delight. "Come on! Come on!"

Eva disappeared from the stairs, her footsteps trailing back to her room. As Elle and I began to climb the staircase, I felt her grip on my hand increase, her face frozen and her eyebrows arched.

"It's okay," I whispered. "She seems...nice. She'll understand."

Elle didn't reply.

"See Louis, I told you they would come!" Eva said with a bursting triumph.

We froze as we listened for a response, yet there was nothing. As the silence sunk in, Eva stuck her head out of the doorway to her bedroom.

"Come look!" she said with a wide grin.

Following her to her bedroom, we stopped in the doorway to view what she'd prepared. By the end of the bed sat a tray with a large blue teapot and a matching set of teacups. There were several pillows arranged in a circle around the offering with three spaces vacant with the remaining three taken up by one of Eva's dolls. Eva stood to the left of it, a hopeful smile on her face as she waited for our reactions.

I was a bit old for tea parties, but looking at Eva's glowing face, I knew I would've been the biggest jerk on the planet if I didn't play along.

"T-this looks great!" I said, bursting with a forced excitement.

Pushing aside any conflicting thoughts, I set myself down on the pillow beside her. She beamed at me before glancing up at Elle who remained by the door, playing with her fingers before taking a step forward to sit across from me at the circle. Eva began pouring the 'tea' from the pot, giving us and the dolls an even serving of nothing.

"I'm sorry I don't have actual tea. I don't know how to work the new big stove," she said. "Father doesn't even know how to use it and it's all he talks about because it cost a lot of money."

"That's okay," I said.

I kept my eyes on Elle, watching as she stared into the empty bowl of her tea cup. She didn't say much as Eva talked more about her dolls, just staring into her cup as if she were hoping something could emerge from it.

"What's that?" Eva asked.

Elle snapped from her daze as Eva pointed to her backpack and the book sticking out from the unzipped pocket.

"The cover's really pretty," Eva said. "Can I?"

Elle gave a slight nod before reaching back to take the book from her backpack, handing it to Eva. I was rather happy to change the conversation from dolls to books, watching with intrigue as Eva flipped through the pages to find the few illustrations that went along with the texts. She squinted, moving her face closer to the paper.

"What are these girls doing?" Eva asked.

I shuffled closer to her, leaning over her shoulder to look at the page. It was one of my favourite pictures in the book, the three main characters running together, swords held high to fight the horde of trolls that came at them.

"Fighting the trolls," I replied, frowning as I thought the picture had made it obvious.

"Why?" Eva asked.

"If they don't stop them, they'll steal their parents—"

"Girls can fight trolls?" Eva asked, keeping her eyes on the page.

I blinked at her, lost as to what to say. Elle shifted towards Eva, all of us now huddled around the book. Elle pinched the pages, flipping through the book to find another illustration.

"Yeah, see?" Elle replied.

Elle pointed at the closing picture of the three girls standing atop of a pile of troll corpses. Thinking back, the scene would've been rather gruesome without the layers of colorful paint and censorship. Yet, Eva still looked confused.

"Um, so do you read much?" I asked Eva, my voice hitching as I tried to distract her.

I was half worried that she'd catch on—that she'd see that we were hiding something. I was a pretty crap liar after all. Even so, the thought of her inevitably asking where the doll was filled me with dread.

"Mother says reading is bad for you," Eva replied.

Elle's shoulders hunched, her eyes falling to the floor. My mind buzzed as I searched for a new topic—a new distraction—anything.

"What do you like to do then?" I asked, "Other than play with dolls?"

Eva's eyes lit up like a Christmas tree. She placed the book down on the floor before climbing to her feet, standing opposite us with a beaming smile.

"I can sing," she said.

A slight relief washed over me as Eva shifted her stance, clasping her hands together just under her chest before twisting her neck towards the open bedroom door.

"Louis!" she called.

There was a moment of pause before piano music drifted from upstairs. My eyes trailed back to Eva as she clasped her hands together in front of her chest, opening her mouth to release an angelic voice. I lowered my tea back into the tray, Eva's voice pulling me into a trance. My attention was locked onto her.

A slight noise interrupted but I didn't care to notice until Eva suddenly stopped, staring down at Elle. I blinked, easing from my trance as the noise grew. I turned towards Elle who'd curled up, her face buried in her hands as she continued to sob softly. Snapping to my senses, I crossed the circle to sit beside her, placing my hand on her shoulder as she curled deeper inwards to hide her face in her knees.

"I never made anyone cry from singing before..." Eva said, blinking down at Elle.

"No, I'm sorry, I just..." Elle replied, wiping her face with her knuckles, "I lost your doll."

Eva's face drew a blank, her face dazed as she waited, Elle sniffling and sobbing into her palms.

"Oh," she murmured.

"Her sister took it, it wasn't her fault," I said, glancing between Elle and Eva, "we'll try and get it back."

I tried to find any signs of anger in Eva's face, finding only a blank slate as she sat down beside Elle. Eva stared at Elle like she was staring at a strange reptile behind glass, reaching forward to push aside the curtain of Elle's hair, her eyes landing on Elle's bruise.

"When you get it back, does that mean you'll come visit again?" she asked.

"Um, sure, yes!" Elle said, jumping at the chance of forgiveness, "and you can keep my book, so you know I mean it."

I glanced back at Eva, my grip on Elle's arm tightening as Eva's expression finally changed. It was only slight, her whitened eyes widening whilst they fixated on us. I swallowed down, a dread draping over me like a heavy blanket as Eva tilted her head slightly.

"Or...you don't ever have to go back."

Her voice was layered with ice. Elle blinked away her tears, gawking at Eva before turning back to me. I opened my mouth to reply, yet the words escaped me. What was I supposed to say to that?

I let out a sharp yelp as a shrill ding echoed through the house, as if someone had smashed their fists against a set of piano keys. Eva stood up, clenching her fists as she turned towards the bedroom door.

"Louis, no!" Eva screamed, her face twisting in frustration. "You're scaring them!"

Snatching Elle's hand, I pulled us both to our feet. I leaned down to grab my backpack as Eva edged towards the door, peeking down the hallway and towards the staircase.

"Quick!" she hissed, waving her arms to gesture at us to follow her.

We spilled into the hallway, my eyes latching onto the first door I saw, the one at the end of the hall. I reached for the doorknob only for my palm to be slapped away. I gawked up at Eva who gazed down at me with sharp, trembling eyes.

"No!" she snapped. "Never go in that room."

She didn't wait for me to reply, stepping towards her mother's room before flinging open the door, and sharply pointing her finger inside. Elle and I remained in place, my eyes drifting towards the staircase and wondering if she could out run us.

There was a sudden thump from the staircase, followed by another, turning into a continuous storm flowing up the steps. Elle and I flew into the mother's bedroom, watching as Eva closed the door behind us, her light footsteps sweeping across the hallway back to her own room. I felt Elle's arms wrap around me, my hands clasping her back as the harder footsteps reached the top of the stairs, trailing towards Eva's room before a gripping silence passed through.

"You ruin everything!" Eva screamed.

"They took it. They must have stolen it!" a voice replied. It was slightly deeper but still bursting with youth.

"I don't care!" Eva replied, "I want them to stay!"

"The only thing you should want or need is me!" the voice replied.

The voice sent spider-like chills running down my body, my chest clenching at its icy tone. Enshrined in Elle's grip, I scanned the bedroom, my eyes setting on the bed. My jaw eased open as I glanced past the bedsheet to find the lump in the bed filled. Instead of a gap there was a body with arms, legs and a face gawking back at us. Their eyes were narrowed and cold, skin worn and aged with ashy-blonde hair trailing across the pillow. I gripped tighter onto Elle as it sat up, revealing its white nightgown, sunken cheeks, translucent skin and blue lips that parted to reveal a swollen, black tongue.

"You brat!" it screamed.

A scream sliced through my throat before I lunged towards the door, gripping Elle's hand as we stumbled into the hallway.

"Wait!" Eva screamed, leaping from her own room as we charged towards the staircase, "Louis, no!"

As we neared the first step, the straps of my backpack dug into my shoulders. We flew backwards and my eyes landed on Elle whose face faded to blankness, her eyes bulging from their sockets. I screamed, unhooking my arms from the straps before I fell to the ground, my knees knocking against the hard-wooden floor.

"Come on!" I screamed at Elle.

With a long leap, I took off down the stairs, the skin of my palm burning against the railing as I staggered down, nearly losing my footing before I finally found the bottom. I flung myself across the foyer and felt the fresh air breathe against my cheek as I began to open the door, only for the knob to jerk against my grip.

"No! No!" I cried.

Charging forwards, I pulled the door handle. The door clipped my heel and sent me tumbling forwards onto the porch, my glasses falling down the veranda stairs. My vision glazed over as I crawled forwards, clutching the frames before shoving them back onto my nose. There was a crack running down the right lens, but it was better than nothing.

I gawked at the darkness that surrounded me. It was night, cold and silent. My heart straining in my tight chest, I stormed down the porch stairs and sprinted across the front yard and out of the gates. My body seared with burning adrenaline as I pushed forward, the trees zipping past me like insects. As I dipped deeper into the forest, my foggy brain began to clear, tiredness straining my eyes. My muscles surged, my stomach flipping as I pulled myself to a stop. My eyes scanned the blackened landscape.

"Elle?" I called, "Elle!"

Silence. I tried again, and again, tearing my throat with each syllable. Tears rolled down my face, sobs filling my throat as I wandered through the darkness.

"Elle, where are you?" I called, "I want to go home, please!"

I paused as a distant rumbling caught my ear, my eyes widening as I recognised the sound of a growling car engine. With a sharp gasp, I took off again, following it until I stumbled upon the road, my sore feet stinging as they slapped the hard asphalt. I kept going, following the distant town lights before I reached the outer neighbourhood streets.

I still didn't know where exactly I was going, my thoughts glazing over again until all I could think of was 'run.' I felt my foot skid against the ground, the wind rushing out from beneath me as I fell forward, the skin of my knees scraping against the rough pavement. I left out a loud sob as pain coursed through me, lifting my hands to see the violent red against my pale skin.

"Oh my god!"

Glancing up, I saw a figure emerge from the shadow of a nearby home. I froze, tears rolling down my face as it all finally caught up to me. The figure stepped into the blinding light of the overhead streetlight, revealing an elderly lady with white hair, wearing a cream-coloured nightgown and slippers. She was towing her rubbish and recycling bins behind her, dropping both as she rushed over to me with open palms. She half bent down beside me. Her old knees probably wouldn't allow her to do anymore. I continued to cry, clawing at the rough pavement as the old lady rubbed my back.

"It's okay, sweetheart," she asked, her voice thin with worry. "What are you doing out here? It's so late, you should be home in bed."

"The, and I, and Elle—I couldn't..."

My thoughts bounced around my head like fireworks, slipping from my grip and exploding as I heaved for breath, my heart pumping hard as I inhaled too much oxygen for my lungs to bear.

"Hold on, look at me, dear," the old lady said, her voice firming as she pressed her palm against my wet cheek, turning my face towards her.

"Oh my god!" she gasped.

"W-what?" I asked.

"It's okay, sweetheart," she said, gripping my shoulders. "Come inside, we'll get you—"

"No!" I screamed, slapping away her hand.

The old lady gawked down at me and her eyes widened as I backed into her fence, curling into a ball to sob into my knees.

"Jack! Get out here!" the old lady called.

"What's the matter?" a voice replied.

"It's one of the girls from the poster, the blonde one!" the old lady gasped.

There was a slight thump before an old man peeked out from behind the fence. He gawked at me for a split second, his eyes widening before he ducked back in.

"Shit, Jenny. She's wearing the same clothes and everything," he said.

I think they forgot I could hear them, my confusion fueling the tremors in my body. Their voices began to haze as a trembling chill overtook me, my mind racing into a dizzy spell until a thick blur glazed over my eyes. I felt the bursting urge to sprint back to the house to get Elle, yet fear swallowed my body and kept me locked in place, trembling like a cornered rabbit.

Jenny rounded the fence, bending down beside me again. My eyes fixated on her, as if she would lunge at me at any moment.

"We're just going to call the police, and they'll get your mummy and daddy to pick you up," she said, smiling as she gave my back a comforting pat. "It's okay now, love."

My frown deepened, my shoulders lifting to reach my ears. I shook my head, tears pouring from my eyes as I squeezed them shut.

"I don't want them... I want Elle."

I didn't say much after that. I was too busy revisiting it, replaying it over and over again inside my head like a VHS tape. I didn't respond to my parents. I let my mother hug me to be nice, although I tensed up like a twisted rag as she did so. My father hovered over her, his face flashing with a tornado of emotions.

"Gone for six months and you've got nothing to say?" my father snapped. "You scared the shit out of us!"

And they were off to the races. My mother spun around and started barking at him about child support. I blocked out the rest, reaching up to massage my neck as a sharp tickle roamed around my throat. Their arguing turned to blur as I thought back to the house, its shadow still consuming me as I fell into a loop of spiraling memories.

"Zoe? Zoe?"

I jerked as a soft hand tapped my shoulder, my eyes darting around the room. It was quiet and my parents sat in chairs on opposite ends of the room, their arms crossed and their eyes averted to separate corners of the space. In front of me stood a soft-faced policewoman with a notepad and pen in hand. *How long had I been gone this time?* I wondered.

Officer Elaine introduced herself and sat down. Her voice was like warm butter, yet I still felt tremors running through my body like a herd of horses. She sat down next to the hospital bed, the scrape of the chair against the floor.

"How are you feeling?" she asked. "Are you thirsty? Would you like some water?"

I glanced over to the white table at the end of the bed. The nurse had placed a glass of water and some snacks for me there, but I hadn't touched them. I pressed my dried lips together, but shook my head 'no.' Officer Elaine smiled at me before sitting down in the chair beside the bed.

"Now we're really happy to have you home, but we still need to bring Elle home," she said. "Could you tell us where you last saw her? You don't have to explain anything, just tell me what you remember seeing or if anyone else was there or..."

I detached from her voice, my eyes falling down to the white covers. The scratch in my throat grew as my lips began to part.

"She's..."

Then it happened again. My eyes glazed over, my lungs burning and my chest tightening as I let out one strangled cough after another, a metallic taste blooming in my mouth. A sing-song voice slipped into my hearing, sending pin-like prickles up my body.

"...quiet..."

"Christ, Zoe," my father snapped. "Can't you just spit it out?"

"What's wrong with her?" my mother replied, standing to pour me a glass of water.

"I'll get the nurse," Officer Elaine replied, rising from her seat. "Maybe she caught something."

My mother placed the glass of water into my hands, the liquid jerking inside the cup as I continued to cough and gag.

"Just drink, okay? It'll help," my mother sighed, sinking back into her seat, gawking at the hospital floor with spread eyes. "What are we going to do? What is everyone going to think?"

I tried to smother the coughs, feeling as if with every choke, I made the tension in the room tighten. I lifted the water to my lips as another cough passed through. I froze, my muscles tensing as I gazed into the cup. From my lips a drop of red had fallen into the water, the red streaking through the translucent liquid before fading as if it were never there. I gawked down at the water, my breath catching in my chest.

"Zoe?"

I lifted my eyes from the cup, meeting my mother's eyes as she gazed back at me, her brow creased. I loosened my grip on the glass before lifting it to my lips, my throat tensing as the liquid poured down my throat.

"Thank you," I mumbled.

She sighed, easing forward to rest her face in her palms, leaving us encased in the cold stillness of silence once again.

Part Four

I **BEGAN COUNTING THE DAYS** since I'd last seen Elle, then months, then years. Then suddenly, it was 2008 and they still couldn't find her. They sent me to god knows how many child psychologists, psychiatrists and specialists that tried to poke and prod at everything I said. They tried hypnotising me once, but I just stared off into the wall. A few months in, one of the lead investigators screamed at me to stop making up stories and wasting his time with all my 'childish tales.' He'd been nice to me for most of the investigation so I think he was just trying the strategy out to see if I would 'snap out of it.' I wouldn't talk to him after that.

The only way I could relay what 'happened' was if I wrote it down in third person. If I tried to speak about it, I would start heaving and coughing, as if my throat was closing up to trap my words inside. My mouth would fill with the taste of sour cherries which slowly turned to metal. Most adults were patient with me for the first couple of tries before telling me to stop overreacting.

Both of my parents weren't too pleased with having to deal with everything. Having the divorce on top of the 'crazy, hallucinating child' was a lot on them, so I made sure not to bother them with it. I didn't go back to school for almost half a year. To be honest, I was hoping everyone would forget who I was and just assume I was new.

My first day of ninth grade was on a rainy day, so my mother had to drive me. I went through my normal routine of dressing myself in clothes that I actually liked, brushing my teeth, shoving a piece of toast down my throat before meeting her at the car. She was on the phone with one of her co-workers and I was grateful. I slid into the front seat, resting my chin in my palm as we pulled out of the garage. After three long years of court proceedings, my mother had kept the house in the divorce along with partial custody of me. She threw a bigger fit over not keeping her brand-new car than she did over not being able to see me on the weekends.

Half-way into town, she got off her phone, just as I reached into my school bag to grab my glasses case, using the soft rag I kept inside to clean my simple black frames. My mother had made her distaste for them very clear when I came home with them months earlier.

"Why won't you wear your contacts?" she asked. "They were really expensive."

I didn't reply, keeping my eyes forward as I counted down the distance towards the school. My mother huffed and started going on one of her typical rants about my 'teenage mood swings.' We finally pulled into the school car park, but I had to wait in the front seat until she was done lecturing me, unlocking the car door. I slipped from the car, slinging my backpack over my shoulder.

"Goodbye, Zoe," my mother called, her eyebrows rising to make her expectation of a response obvious.

I gave her a dead stare, her eyelids heavy and my lips limp as I weighed my temptation to slam the door in her face against the inevitable tantrum she'd throw if I did. I couldn't be bothered.

"Bye," I muttered.

I felt a few stray eyes latch onto me as I crossed the front yard. I tried to convince myself that it was because I'd cut my hair over the break, my blonde locks shaped into a short pixie cut. Yet an overbearing awareness crawled up my back, my shoulders hunching as I entered the main building.

There were people who thought I'd done it. That Elle's body was hidden in the forest somewhere, and the police were waiting for me to crack. Elle and I had kept to ourselves, so there was plenty of room for mystery. It's amazing the stories people were willing to make up about two shy eleven-year-old girls. News reporters and such came to the house for months until the story died. My father rushed inside once after school, as they swarmed us like vultures to carrion. I covered my ears and closed my eyes, unwilling to open them even as we were locked in the house.

Elle's parents didn't help. The police turned to them pretty quickly after I told them about the purple patch on Elle's face. A brick flew through my bedroom window the day after Jess was removed from their custody, but she was back by the same weekend. As the heat turned on them, they tried to conjure up even more fire to throw at me. I thankfully never heard a word of what they said from any adult, but the kids at school were like echo chambers for their parents. I'll never forget the day when a glossy-eyed eight-year-old walked up to me on my first day of sixth grade to ask, *"Is it true you eat bats and pull off their wings?"*

Some asked me why I didn't cry, why I didn't want to talk about it, why I wouldn't do a press interview or why I couldn't even hear about it without having to leave the room.

Maybe they were right. Maybe I was lying or confused. Maybe I did just make it up because I was a child stuck in a fantasy world. What if it actually didn't happen at all, or what if it happened to someone else? I let all these questions and thoughts flow through me until I felt as if I were floating in a sea of them.

I retreated to the distilled silence of the library, tucking myself into one of the tables at the back, surrounded by the bookcases. Setting my backpack on the floor beneath me, tugging out my latest read before setting it on the table. Adjusting my glasses, I began to read, time lulling to a stop around me as I was absorbed into the pages.

"Hey Zoe."

My eyes flew up from the page, darting across the room until they landed on the owner of the voice. My startled heart calmed, but only slightly as Tina beamed back at me. I was taller than her now, yet I felt so small around her in a strange, warm way.

"How was debate last night?" I asked.

Tina crossed the small space between the bookshelves, setting her stack of books down next to me before sliding into her seat. I felt my posture straighten and a smile come naturally to my lips.

"Great! We qualified for the state championship next month," she said, huffing in slight amusement, "my dad nearly lost his mind, though. You'd think I'd just won the World Cup or something."

I felt a lump grow in my throat, my eyes falling back to my book to flip the page as I failed to find an image of my own father being so excited for me. Tina turned to me, tilting her head as her eyes lit up in acknowledgement.

"Love the new frames," she said, reaching to tap her finger against my glasses, "we almost match now."

"Er, yeah," I said, smiling through the slight heat that rose in my cheeks.

Tina beamed back at me, tucking her black hair behind her ear. She had several piercings now, two in each lobe and a single crescent moon-shaped stud in her upper ear. I went with her to get it done for her fifteenth birthday. I'd pointed out the moon earring and she chose it. *'What do you think?'* she asked afterwards. I only glanced at the earring for a second before my eyes landed back on her face, *'...beautiful'* I replied. *'Thanks,'* she said pausing slightly, *'means a lot coming from you.'*

"Hey, can I ask you a favour?" Tina said.

"Yeah..." I replied, flipping my book closed.

Tina pulled out her chair so that she was properly facing me, I felt my body tense with a warm nervousness.

"So, one of the editors of the school newspaper has come down with something. I didn't ask, but he sounded like shit over the phone. So, I was wondering if you could help us cover the inter school sports tournament?" she asked.

"Um, er... sure!" I replied.

Tina's face lit up, her arms flinging open as she crashed into me, pulling me into a tight hug. It felt so right having her in my arms. I'd spent many long nights wondering why it felt that way, like a perfect puzzle-piece slipping into place.

"Oh my god! Thank you! You've saved my ass," she said, locking her arms around my shoulders, "I already have so much to do with debate and tutoring, and I've my sister's wedding this weekend, and I—"

I spaced out a bit as she rambled on, waiting for the blush to die in my cheeks before I tuned into her rant. She was always overworking herself in an attempt to keep up with her burning ambition. As much as I liked how passionate she was, she needed help slowing down.

"It's okay," I interrupted, "I got it; it's taken care of."

Tina let out a long breath before leaning away from me, a slight smile spreading across her face.

"Thanks Zoe," she said.

Her face began to wilt, as if a sudden thought had torn her from her relief. A seed of concern sprouted within me as she reached to place her hand on my shoulder.

"Hey, so I heard you were... um...stopped by some TV people the other day," Tina said.

My lips parted, my eyes retreating to the corner of the room.

"Well yeah, some new 'unsolved mysteries' thing apparently," I replied, my heart picking up at a quicker pace at the thought of it, "I hid in the grocery store until they left."

I glanced down to my lap, giving my head a light shake, as if to knock the memory from my head, yet it stuck like glue.

"Do you want someone to walk home with you?" Tina asked, her eyebrows arching in concern, "my house is on the way so if someone does try something, you can call your dad or whatever from there."

I paused. After Elle...I always walked home by myself. I never invited anyone and never ventured near the forest. This would be the first time someone had joined me. As much as the idea set me off, I kept my eyes on Tina.

"Um, okay." I replied.

"Thank god the rain stopped," Tina said.

Tina normally went to one of the local cafés or the park with her other friends after school. She waved to them as we left the school grounds. She knew not to take the route towards the forest, although the trees still loomed over the houses like dark clouds on the horizon.

"Hey, um, thanks for walking back with me," I said.

"No worries," she replied with a calming smile, "I need to get in some studying, plus I've spent all my allowance on that new chocolate slice they have at…"

I could listen to her talk for hours, but we eventually sunk into a comfortable silence, passing by each house at a leisurely pace. I felt a slight tightness in my chest as I let one hand fall from my backpack strap. I let it hang for a minute before I built up the courage to brush my fingers against Tina's knuckles. She tilted her head slightly towards me so I tried again, only for her to catch my hand like a fish from the river. I kept my eyes forward as I tried to hide the blush on my cheeks, adjusting my grip on Tina's hand as we continued on. It was as if firecrackers were going off in my stomach. I felt so high, but the nervousness made me feel borderline sick. Yet I never wanted to let go. I swallowed back my embarrassment to gaze at her from the corner of my eye. She was smiling at me, giving my hand a light squeeze. I glanced forward again, a light smile spreading across my face as Tina chuckled.

"Hey um," I said, my heart pounding in my chest, "you thought about prom?"

Prom was months away still but it had been on the forefront of my mind. Mum had been hounding me about getting a dress and a date and Grandma was always telling me I needed to find a compromise with her. So, I won't do the dress but I'll do the date part, even though it would not be the kind Mum wanted.

"Oh shit," Tina said, "I've been so busy I completely forgot. Dad would lose it if I brought a boy though."

I took in a deep breath, heat rushing to my cheeks as I gathered up my courage. It was now or never.

"W-would it be okay if you brought me instead?"

We stopped as Tina turned towards me, her eyes widened with shock. I felt my stomach drop. Had I completely misread all of it? I opened my mouth to take it back, to retreat back into the box I'd tried to peek outside of. Yet, my words caught in my throat as a smile spread across Tina's face.

"Yeah, he likes you," she said, "and...I wasn't really interested in taking a guy anyway."

I gawked back at her as she resumed walking, dragging me forward by my hand like I'd just asked her to. It took me a moment to realise that she'd seen me and hadn't flinched away. The relief made my head spin, like I'd been carrying around a massive metal shield that I could finally put down. I couldn't wipe the smile off my face when it finally sunk in that I was taking Tina, smart, confident, pretty Tina, to the prom.

Then it came again, just as I knew it would. Memories of all the days I would walk home with Elle. They'd always pop up, almost like a reminder that I wasn't allowed to be happy. Not while Elle was still missing. My grip loosened from Tina's hand as my thoughts flew backwards to what seemed like distant, almost transparent memories. Tina must've thought I was just shy as she gave my hand another light squeeze before tugging me closer to her so that our shoulders brushed against one another. I bit back a blush, yet tried to cling to the moment so I wouldn't fall backwards into the darkness again. We walked in a comfortable silence until we reached Tina's place.

"This is me," she said, stepping from the pavement but keeping a grip on my hand, "will you be okay?"

"Yeah, thanks," I said.

"Would it be okay if I told Dad we're going to prom?"

I smiled despite the hesitation. People were going to find out anyway, people were probably already whispering about it, hence Mum's desperation to prove them wrong. Might as well be on my terms that the rumour is confirmed. Plus, I was happy for Tina that she felt okay enough telling her dad.

I gave a gentle nod, prompting Tina to smile and run her thumb over my knuckles before releasing my hand.

"See you tomorrow?" she said.

"Sure," I replied.

I watched as she crossed her front lawn, brushing off her shoes on the doormat before slipping inside. I lingered for a moment, feeling my hand grow cold again before setting off.

"Hey!" a voice called, "have time for your adoring fans, freak?"

I froze, warmth draining from my limbs as I glanced over my shoulder. I don't remember their names. I think one started with an 'S' and the other was something like 'Emma' or 'Emily' or something like that. They were in Jess' grade, I knew, and they loved to shout shit at me if I ever crossed their path on school grounds. Regardless, I continued to walk, hoping my silence would bore them enough to leave me alone as usual. I quaked as I heard footsteps follow after me, a chill drawing down my spine.

"Aw what? Don't have time for us, got an interview or something?" S said.

I bit my lip, my eyes searching the streets for some kind of escape. I thought of bolting, but it was a straight street without any kind of turn. I could run that far, and fast, but I wasn't sure if I could out run them or their fists.

"Just leave me alone," I told them.

I felt a hand lock onto my shoulder, air whipping through my close-cropped hair as I was spun around, my feet slapping against the pavement as I regained my balance. Emma had her hands in her pockets and an ironed expression whilst S was smiling, her hands on her hips and her posture slightly bent forward.

"How much do you have on you?" S asked.

Fifty dollars if I recalled correctly, shoved into the bottom of my backpack in case of emergencies, but if I opened my backpack, they'd probably just grab the whole thing, including my assignments, homework and textbooks. Bruises are easy to fix, but I didn't want to have to swallow my pride and ask either of my parents for more money for school things.

"Nothing," I lied.

S raised her eyebrows, smiling in a sarcastic disbelief. She glanced at Emma who kept her stone-cold eyes locked onto me.

"Nothing?" Emma asked.

"Yeah, didn't you hear me?" I asked, deepening my voice slightly.

I must have looked like a tiny kitten trying to let out a roar because the two of them burst into manic laughter. My shoulders hunched as the embarrassment sunk in, my eyes dropping to the pavement.

"Is that how to fend off the ghosts or monsters or whatever?" Emma cackled.

My stomach plummeted, my jaw slacking as S turned to Emma mid-chuckle.

"Nah, probably a wendigo or something— that's why they can't find a body," she said.

"You're fucking disgusting!" I spat, my face twisting in a bursting anger.

"Ooooh, what's wrong?" S said with a grin, "that didn't sound very innocent of you. I bet you fucking skinned her something."

I felt a pulse of rage run through me, as my hand flew into the air, my palm bursting with a sharp pain. S stood with a blank expression and a reddened cheek, blinking away her confusion before turning to gawk at me. Emma stepped forward, her clenched fist aimed at me. I let out a strangled yelp as I was pulled backwards, my feet slipping out from beneath me as I landed flat against the pavement, the skin of my palms tearing against the rough surface. Glancing up, I saw a figure charge past me, their knuckles meeting Emma's cheekbone.

"Jess, what the fuck?" S screamed.

"Want to say that about my sister again?" Jess growled.

S leaped backwards, her eyes widened as she dodged Jess' fist. Emma stood bent over, her hands cradling her face as she groaned in pain.

Snapping from my shock, my senses returned like a crashing wave. Pushing myself off the ground, I broke into a sprint. My feet slapped against the pavement as my eyes fixated on my path, my heart drumming in my ears as the shouting behind me grew quieter. I didn't think of where to run. I just ran, my nippy legs carrying me down the road. I didn't stop until the fresh smell of pine hit my nose, prompting me to skid to a stop. Ahead of me was the road that outlined the forest, behind me was the road back to S, Emma and Jess. I sure as hell wasn't going back.

Gripping the straps of my backpack, I followed the circling road, keeping my eyes forward instead of the trees that reached out to me with their arm-like branches. I picked up my pace, the shadows of the trees hovering over me, as if ready to pluck me from the road and drag me back once again.

"Zoe!"

A sudden screech tore through the afternoon silence, a yelp bursting from my mouth as I leapt to my right, my feet meeting the dirt of the forest floor. The car skidded to a halt next to me, the window already half way down. I almost didn't recognise the driver as he stuck his head out, grey sprouting from his short locks and his forever unamused expression now marked with wrinkles. I was at first relieved to see my father, but it was as short-lived as his marriage.

"What are you doing out here? School's over," he said.

My fear quickly burned into anger, my eyes sharpening as sweat formed along my hairline.

"And?" I asked, raising my palms slightly.

He blinked at me, his eyebrows dropping as a slight surprise painted his face. He scoffed, shaking his head as if he was bored of me.

"Wow, I guess they're right about mothers and daughters," he muttered.

"At least she'd pay child support on time," I replied.

He rolled his eyes at that.

"Just get back before dark or she'll be calling me looking for you," he spat.

With a growling huff, he settled back into his seat, rolling up the window as he sped off in a sudden jolt. I growled, anger still bubbling in my veins as I watched the car disappear down the road.

"Wow, did your balls finally drop, Princess?"

Twisting around, I found Jess standing with her arms crossed and a swollen nose, streaks of blood running across her upper lip from when she wiped it with her sleeve. I bowed my head, shuffling my feet before giving up on forming a response.

I set down my backpack, opening it to find a travel pack of tissues sitting at the bottom next to my pencil case. I rose to my feet before extending the tissues towards her. She frowned, glancing between the packet and then back at me before another jewel of blood fell from her nose. She sighed before stepping forward, taking the packet from me before tearing a tissue from it. We stood in silence as she pressed the tissue to her nose. I was her height now, both of us standing evenly at five foot nine. I noted that I liked her band shirt but was too shy to tell her. I felt the temptation to leave, but I couldn't stop staring at her face, her freckles, her brown eyes and dark hair. I couldn't help but wonder what Elle would look like.

Jess cleared her throat before tucking the bloody tissue into her jeans pocket.

"The least you owe me," she said, grinding the heel of her shoe against the road, "I just kicked the shit out of my only friends for you."

"What do you want, Jess?" I asked.

Jess cocked her eyebrow, taking a large step towards me.

"What were you trying so bloody hard to prove back there?" she asked, "that you're tough, that you're not Mummy and Daddy's little girl?"

Anger reignited in me, my foot lunging with my hands poised to shove her. Jess' eyes flashed, my body flinched backwards as she lurched forwards, pointing her chin towards me. I froze like a rabbit under the gaze of a fox.

"Don't even think about it, unless you want to get bitch-slapped again," she replied through gritted teeth, "are you going to answer me? What are you trying to prove?"

"Why does it matter?" I spat.

Jess leaned on her left foot, tucking her hands in her pockets as she poked the inside of her cheek with her tongue before turning back to me.

"I don't know... I'm just wondering if it has anything to do with Elle," she replied.

There was such venom in her words, enough to send a chill down my spine. My glasses slipped down my nose as I lifted my chin slightly to stare at her, surprised at what I saw. Yet her eyes told a different story. They were sharp and aimed at me like a pair of knives, yet under a glassy coat lay a softness, a hurt that pulsed through her.

"What happened that day?" she asked.

Automatically, the itch started in my throat, a cough lodging in my lungs as if warning me to stay silent.

"I've already told—"

"No, I mean what actually happened, none of that bullshit about a house, or whatever," she said, jabbing a finger towards me, "it's been four years, nearly fucking five! Don't you think I deserve a damn explanation?"

"You didn't even care about her!" I spat, regretting each word as it fell out of my mouth, "all you cared about were your friends and throwing paint at us for fun!"

"Says you, you were the spoiled little bitch with her head up her ass," Jess roared, "what good were you to her, to anyone?"

My hand found the strap of my bag, my arm bending as I threw it at Jess, my anger still hot in my body as it struck her in the chest. Jess didn't hesitate like the other two— I felt her hands grip onto my flannel shirt, my body flying forward as she pulled me towards her. Her eyes were wide and her nostrils flaring.

"You must be really stupid, you—"

A groan tore through her throat as I kicked her in the shin, charging forward to send us both to the ground. My glasses tumbled from my face, and my vision went blurry as I braced myself against the floor with Jess' body beneath me. I gasped as I felt her knee lodge into my stomach, my body solidifying like a rock. Air rushed by me as she knocked me to the ground, my back slamming into the dirt before I felt her punch land hard against my face. My nose exploded with a piercing pain, a searing heat spreading across my skin. I screamed, clasping my hand over my mouth as I squeezed my eyes shut. I groaned into my palms, trying to will away the pain whilst bracing for another punch. To my shock, it didn't come. Instead I felt a small splat of liquid falling against my knuckle. Peeking through the blinds of my fingers, I gawked up at Jess. Her swelling eyes were a bloodshot red, her face twisted into a tight expression and her fist clenched and ready for strike again.

A pulse of fear rushed through me as I took a hand from my mouth, lashing my open palm towards her. I yelped as Jess gripped my wrist, slamming it into the ground. I winced, my anger swelling once again as I twisted beneath her grip.

She panted through gritted teeth, her fist trembling as if desperate to reach me. Yet, she remained stiff and frigid, tears spilling from her face. Guilt hit me like a boulder to the chest, settling in my stomach. I didn't know what to say, gawking as she climbed off of me.

"Fucking hell," Jess sobbed, giving her face another hard wipe before turning to me, "don't you ever try to fight someone, okay? You're shit at it. They'll kill you without even trying."

I still don't know what I could've said to that. Despite her blunt words, I felt a slight warmth attached to them. It was kind of like that foul, liquorice-tasting medicine you have to take when you're sick, hard to swallow but it made me feel better. I waited, watching as she continued to pour out her emotions that I'd cruelly thought she didn't have.

I pushed myself up onto my elbows, my head throbbing as more tears trailed down my blotchy cheeks. I blinked as Jess' hand hovered in front of my face, my glasses hanging loosely in her grip. I glanced at her, but she stared straight ahead. I took them, flinching as she snapped back her hand.

"But then what am I supposed to do?" I asked.

"Do I look like I have all the answers for you?" Jess sighed harshly.

Jess drew in her legs, locking her arms over her knees as she curved her spine. I put on my glasses, the crack only slightly jarring my vision. I sighed, winching at my throbbing nose and lips.

"I don't want to be a coward anymore," I said.

"Who said you were a coward?"

I laid there for a minute, trying to soak in what she'd said. After a while, I pushed myself up to sit, rubbing my hands against my jeans to brush off the dirt. I wanted to cry. I waited for it, but like every other time, it just wouldn't come. No matter how much I craved such a release. Reaching up, I slipped my fingers past my lips, running them across my gums before pulling them out. Red coated my fingertips, the liquid glistening against the light, like cherries.

"Do you still have that doll?" I asked.

I hadn't been back to Elle's house since that last day. It didn't look much different, except everything seemed so much smaller despite being layered with a bitter nostalgia. Jess told me to wait outside so I stood on the porch, teasing the soles of my shoes against the floor as Jess stepped inside, the door almost closed before a loud voice sounded through the walls.

"Where the hell were you? Do you have the groceries?"

"Yeah," Jess sighed.

Through the crack in the door, I could see Jess unsheathe her backpack, unloading the few contents inside onto the kitchen bench.

"Where's the rest?" the voice asked.

"This as much as I could get. You didn't give me enough to pay for it all," Jess replied.

"I'm sorry, Jess, but that's not my fault," the voice snapped.

I stepped closer towards the door, leaning down to peep further into the kitchen. Jess' mother stood by the stairs, adjusting her black work uniform as she fumbled for her keys.

"Just make sure the dishes are done, and the washing, and have dinner ready for your father when he comes home."

"Can't he make it himself?" Jess asked, her voice somewhat meek before it fell back into its normal blunt tone, "I have homework and he's at the pub anyway, he won't even be home for dinner."

"I don't have time for your attitude, Jessica," her mother replied, "I swear to god, you're almost eighteen, you should know not to talk back with this bullshit—"

I didn't catch what else her mother said, or rather, yelled because I slipped into my head where several questions tugged me in different directions. *Should I do something? If so, then what? Would I make it worse? Should I just do what Jess said and stay outside?*

"I swear to god, you're so fucking worthless, Jess!"

I nearly stumbled on the door as I pushed myself inside, silence following me as two pairs of eyes latched onto me. I took in a smooth breath, my heart thrumming in my chest as I glanced between Jess and her mother.

"What is she doing here?" Jess' mother spat, narrowing her eyes towards me.

"School project," I lied.

Tucking my hands into my pockets, I crossed the kitchen to stand next to Jess. She kept her eyes forward, not acknowledging me at all. I don't really blame her— she was probably embarrassed.

"You're going to be late," she mumbled.

"I hope you're bloody proud of yourself," Jess' mother replied, fixing her hands on her hips, "both of you. The shit you do just to spite me."

I bit my lip, loosening my stance slightly as I glanced off into the corner of the room, biting back any reactive anger that bubbled within me.

"We're talking about this later," Jess' mother said.

With a huff, she gathered up her bag and jacket, storming towards the door before slamming it with a hard thud.

Silence encased the room, the awkwardness thickening the air. I glanced at Jess once again, her expression hidden by the curtain of her hair. She let out a rough sigh before walking towards the stairs, leaving me to follow her.

"...I told you to wait outside," she said.

"You did the same for me earlier," I replied.

Jess paused, glancing over her shoulder to stare down at me from the higher step. I felt my form tense as her eyes fell on me. I couldn't read her at all— I couldn't tell if she was pissed off, apathetic, or neither. She eventually turned and continued up the stairs. Once at the top, I halted as my eyes locked onto the closest door. It was painted white but beneath a thin layer of paint sat a row of black letters that read:

'ELLE'

"Wait here," Jess said, continuing down the hallway to what I assumed was her bedroom.

I glanced back to the door, using the toe of my shoe to nudge the door open. The room on the other side was completely bare, with white walls and a blue-ish carpet. There was no bed, no clothes or personal items. It was as if Elle had never even been there, as if she'd been wiped away. I tucked my hands into my pockets as I leaned into the room, starting to picture together what it may have looked like. What kind of bedsheets, maybe green? Did she have any posters on the walls? Did she have any teddy bears or stuffed animals on her bed? My eyes began to itch, my teeth grinding against one another as I bit back my anger. I took in a deep breath, holding it within me like a swelling fire before breathing out.

I stepped from the room as I heard the door down the hallway close, revealing Jess as she carried a wide box in her arms.

"They sold most of her stuff after Dad lost his job— not that there was much anyway," Jess said, "but I kept a few things."

Jess rested the box on the railing of the staircase, flipping open the lid for me to look inside. There were a few crayon drawings, some stray pieces of Elle-sized clothing and a few books, some of them from our primary school library that were never returned. Not that anyone would be cruel enough to push for a missing girl's books back. The doll sat on top of it all, looking untouched with her green dress perfectly smoothed and woollen hair untangled. Jess picked it up, her firm lips trembling as she gazed down at the smiling face.

"I-I kept brushing its hair and stuff, so it would be waiting for her when she came back," she said, giving the doll's body a light squeeze.

"Why did you take it?" I asked.

Jess blinked, parting her lips before muttering.

"I thought it was yours."

A question came to the front of my mind, a question that had been bouncing through my head for years.

"Do you think, even now, Elle and I would've still been friends?" I asked.

"I don't know," Jess replied, "you never asked any questions. I don't know if you were too dumb to ask or something but...she was never embarrassed around you."

Jess glanced back at the doll, her eyes latching onto it. Her eyes were so raw, yet still made of steel. I didn't dare break the silence.

"That day, when you two left, I was cleaning the kitchen..." Jess said, "I wish I'd told her that...I loved her or whatever."

I searched my head for a reply, yet none came to mind. She wasn't talking to me, or at least, not directly. I was just a person to bounce the words off of so they wouldn't fade.

"I was scared. Even if she magically appeared right now, I don't think I could force the words out. Three words... and I'm so fucking scared of them."

At last, she gazed up at me, her eyes glazed with tears, but still hard as stone. Seething with bitterness, she held the doll out towards me. I lifted my hand to take its tiny, plush arm, but Jess did not release it, holding me in place with that icy stare.

"If you ever decide to tell anyone what really happened, it better be me, not some news people or whatever for some quick buck," she said.

The want to tell her was immediate, my jaw slacking as I prepared the words. Yet, I felt that tickle in my throat again, another warning. I let out a slight cough to clear it before lowering my eyes to the carpet.

"Okay," I said.

Jess waited, letting out a short sigh before letting go of the doll. I brought it to my chest, squeezing it tight as I glanced back up at her.

"And I'm sorry about your face," she muttered, "your lip looks swollen as fuck so you should probably get some ice or something."

I reached up to tap my fingertips against my lip, where it was tender and slightly painful beneath my touch.

"I'm sorry I threw my bag at you... and said that stuff, and pissed you off when I was a kid," I replied.

Jess gave an unamused huff, giving her head a slight shake before resting her hands on her hips. Yet, her face was soft, almost tired as she stared into the pale wall beside her.

"No one's perfect, Princess," she said, "so stop feeling so damn sorry for yourself."

The moment I got to my mother's house, I rushed to the bathroom, dropping my bag on the tiles before clutching onto the sink. My stomach turned like a clogged washing machine, my eyes watering as I stared down the dark drain. With a short gasp of breath, I glanced up into the mirror, taking off my glasses as I gazed at my wide-eyed reflection. My throat clenched as I let out another cough, covering my face with my hands to contain it before reaching to turn on the tap. I splashed handfuls of cold water against my face, trying to snap myself out of this spiral of nausea and short breaths.

My knuckles turned as white as the basin as I raised my gaze to the mirror, my blood running colder than the water as I saw a young girl staring back at me. Barely eleven years old, with a sharp blonde bob and glasses. I yelped, tossing my glasses against the countertop as I turned to the shower. Turning on the faucet, I began to strip as the water ran warm. I huddled in the bottom of the tub, heaving with several dry coughs echoing through the small bathroom. I let the warm droplets of water hit my back, trying to find some form of comfort in their encasing warm.

The thoughts attacked me again. Why was I still alive? Why wasn't I left behind? Why did I deserve to escape? Why did Eva let me go?

Another wave of nausea gripped me, prompting me to clutch the side of the shower, knocking over my mother's expensive shampoo in the process. I heaved, cupping my mouth as the water soaked my hair. I paused as something small and solid smacked the surface of my palm.

At first, I thought I'd coughed up a tooth, due to the red fleshy matter attached to its brownish surface. It wasn't until I turned it over in my fingers that I realised that it was a single cherry pit. I flinched, the pit falling from my grip and trailing down the drain.

I remained on all fours, staring at the bottom of the bathtub with water still raining down on me. The tickle in my throat remained, yet I couldn't cough or gag again. Rising from the curtain of water, I turned off the showerhead, crawling from the tub. The usual reminders ran through my head.

No one believes me. No one will listen to me. I'm the quiet kid who sits at the back of class. I'm the spoiled little girl who couldn't save her best friend. I'm the pathetic freak who makes up stories about dolls, tea parties and houses.

I lifted my gaze to the mirror, my eyes fixated on the reflection that gawked back at me. She looked just over fifteen years old. She had short blonde hair that tickled the top of her earlobes, thick eyebrows and blood-shot green eyes. Her cheeks were blotchy, she had a few zits across her forehead and a tiny dent in her nose that held up her glasses. She looked so scared, so alone.

Trembling and soaked, I began to wonder. *Am I brave or a coward? Am I strong, even if I pretend to be, or am I weak? Do I lock it all away and carry it around on my back, or do I let it loose and see if it'll eat me alive*? I still don't know the answers to half of those questions.

Part Five

MY SKIN PRICKLED, AS IF a thousand tiny needles were piercing through each layer. A lump was swelling in my throat as my weightless legs carried me through the night. I still don't know what I was thinking. I told no one where I was going. I hadn't even called Tina to tell her I couldn't help with the school newspaper after all. I'd emptied my backpack of school supplies and filled it with bottled water, some random snacks from the pantry, the doll and a kitchen knife. I just wanted to reach that house before I ran out of the insanity fuelling me. I'd decided that it was now or never. I was going to bring Elle home.

I'd grown several feet since I last entered the forest, yet I felt even smaller beneath the shadows of the trees. My eyes darted from branch to branch as I powered forward, my face hot, cold sweat running down my cheek. A tiny voice in my head screamed at me to turn around, run home and hide under my covers but through salty tears, I muttered under my breath,

"Keep going, keep fucking going."

I listened for Eva's voice, crying or singing, yet all I could hear was the soft rustling of the trees. I growled in frustration as my surroundings bled into one under the veil of night. I strained my neck, glancing up as I scanned the darkness, my eyes desperate for anything to cling onto. Then I caught it, so very distant but still vibrant amongst the black. The tiny star-like light flickering from the window.

I picked up into a run, my path fixated towards the light. As the forest floor began to incline, it began to take shape: the roof, the walls and the iron gate. A switch suddenly flipped in my body. My bottled-up hesitation rushed through me as I skidded to a halt beneath the shadow of the iron gates. I peered past the gates and up the house. I remembered sprinting out of the front door, the years since shrinking to feel as if I'd only just scampered down those porch steps. I released a shaky breath as I forced my foot forward, stepping past the threshold and into the front yard. I listened for Eva's voice, Elle's sob, or a plaintive piano note, but all I could hear was the crunching of the ground beneath my boots.

I began to tremble as I reached the porch, my hands reaching to rub my upper arms as I approached the door. It was smaller than I remembered, the doorknob tiny in my grip. I took in a deep breath before I clenched the cold metal, giving it a hard twist before swinging open the door. Nothing.

My heart clenched in my chest as I pulled the door closed before opening it once again. Nothing. No foyer, no staircase, just the crumbling remains of an old house. Panic rushed through me, tears pricking my eyes as I slammed the door closed. I paced the porch, my palms clamped on either side of my head as my mind burned with panic.

"Elle! Elle!" I screamed, turning back to the front door, "please! I came back, I'm here!"

I was met with silence, my heartbeat meeting the pace of my racing mind. I ran out to the front yard, glancing up to the second-story as I rummaged through my bag, my fingers finding the soft plush of the doll.

"Eva!" I called, holding the doll up to the house, "I have it! You want it back, don't you? You want to play?"

I paused, holding up the plush offering before my eyes widened. Eva's soft song drifted through my ears, soothing any anger as it attempted to pull me into a daze. I fought it, keeping the doll aimed in the air as I tried to block the numbing tune.

A slight creak interrupted the song, my eyes falling back to the door as it slid open, a warm light spilling from the doorframe. I tucked the doll back into my backpack before approaching the door, a shudder running down my body before I stepped inside.

To my surprise, nothing in the foyer seemed smaller. Twisting around, I found the door towering over me, my fingers barely able to cover the doorknob. My heart thrummed in my chest as I slid the doll into my backpack, pulling out the knife and locking it in my grip. Strapping my backpack on, I peeked into the dining room. The feast was still laid out on the table, untouched and still glistening under the contrasting shadow of the fireplace.

I froze in the doorway, my grip tightening around the knife as I spotted a large figure standing in front of the fireplace, gazing up at the ripped portrait. He stood at just over six foot with a stocky build, his figure cloaked in black.

"H-hey," I said.

My muscles clenched as he turned to face me. He wore a three-piece navy suit, which was made to look expensive yet so plain. His hair was black like Eva's, combed back to reveal a retreating hairline. Also, like Eva, and who I assumed was her mother, his skin was a chalky white with blue veins running up his neck. His white eyes landed on me, my breath catching in my throat as what I originally thought was a goatee began to glisten against the light. He didn't seem bothered by the blood that ran down his chin and neck, or maybe he just never noticed.

"Where's my friend?" I asked.

He raised a bushy eyebrow at me, another layer of black blood falling down his chin as he opened his mouth to speak.

"What are you wearing?" he asked, "are you from the village, or from some land that allows young ladies to dress in such a horrid way?"

I scrunched my nose at the sight of the blood, my form tensing as I tried to contain the burst of anger that rushed through me.

"Where's Elle?" I asked.

"You mean my daughter?" he replied.

"Not Eva, Elle," I replied, my frustration building, "dark hair, freckles, brown eyes!"

"Oh," he mused, his voice still light without a hint of seriousness, "I thought she was the new scullery maid, but no, it seems as if my children have found themselves a new hobby."

"What are you talking about?" I asked.

"My son is practically worthless, you see, so I'm glad that he's got something to do so he won't be as much of a nuisance," he muttered, "at least Eva has some use if I can find someone that'll marry her."

"I mean Elle, you bastard!" I barked, straightening my elbow to extend the knife further.

That got his attention, his posture stiffening as I aimed the edge of the blade at him. He raised his hands, palms facing me as he edged back towards the fireplace.

"What kind of madwoman are you?" he asked, panic rushing through his voice.

His response slapped me with shock. I didn't expect much from pointing a knife at him, I wouldn't've been surprised if he laughed. I was relieved to see him afraid but I couldn't avoid the question. He knew he was dead, right?

"I'm not going to ask again!" I spat.

I tried to let my rage take over, trying to force the reins into its red hands. Yet, I couldn't move, my pounding heart straining my still chest. I couldn't help it. My limbs reflected my resolve, the knife shaking in my trembling grip. I bit down on my lip, my joints locking as I couldn't push forward. For once in my life, I had the power over someone and I didn't want to use it.

He gazed back at me, squinting his eyes before a relieved smile came over his face, a set of black teeth peeping from his ashy lips.

"You won't hurt me," he chuckled, "you're practically worthless. You can't even help yourself, let alone this friend of yours."

My feet remained glued to the floor, my calves tensing as I tried to step towards him. I narrowed my vision, sharpening eyes in place of my lowered knife.

"Fucking watch me," I replied.

Puffing my chest and tightening my lips, I turned on my heels, storming from the room. I wasn't getting anything out of that clueless jerk. I clasped my hand over my face, trembling with frustration before I turned to find him gone, along with the feast, leaving only the empty table.

My mind scrambled for an explanation before a slight *ding* caught my attention. I turned towards the piano as it began to hum a deep tune, freezing as I found a figure seated on the stool. Squeezing the handle of the knife, I stepped towards the living room, sliding my foot across the floorboards.

"Are you finished squawking like a strangled chicken?" he asked.

His calmness threw me off, even his father looked somewhat surprised to see me whilst he passed me off like an everyday insect flying past him.

"Who are you?" I asked.

He finished off the last page before twisting around on the stool. He had messy blond hair that reached the tops of his ears but his father's bushy brows. His eyes were the same as the others', white as summer clouds with matching skin. His face dropped when my eyes fell towards his neck, the skin from his jaw downwards a black-ish purple in contrast to the paleness of his face. Even with his ghostly appearance, my best guess regarding his age was fourteen or fifteen years old.

"Louis Mortimer," he said.

"Eva's...brother?" I asked.

"Yes," he replied, "did she let you in?"

I narrowed my eyes as he turned around to play once again, his back facing me.

"Yeah," I replied, taking another step towards the piano, "I'm Elle's friend,"

He tilted his head as his fingers ran across the keys, my frustration rising in my chest, burning away into anger.

"Oh, you're the one with the annoying scream," he replied.

My eyes flashed red, my free hand lashing forward to grip the piano cover, slamming it closed with a hard swipe. Louis paused, glancing down at his fingers, now jammed between the wooden piano cover and the keys. His expression tensed, taking in a long, sharp breath in through his nose before lifting his eyes towards me. Regret flushed my body as his gaze entrapped me, my hand lifting to aim the edge of the knife towards him. He chuckled at me, the darkness in his eyes remaining despite the glee in his smile.

"I don't know why you're bothering with that," he said.

I flinched as his hand lashed out, latching onto the blade with a tight grip. My eyes widened as he applied pressure, the knife bending to his strength. I struggled to keep my elbow straight as he curved the knife downwards, releasing his grip to reveal his untouched palm clean of any blood or wound.

"I know what I am," he said, "and unlike my parents, I'm not afraid to accept it."

"You're fucking insane!" I spluttered, a nauseating concoction of disgust and fear rushing through me.

Louis huffed in amusement, turning to lean his back against the piano keys.

"Why are you so angry?" he asked.

"Why do you think?" I spat.

He gave a slight shrug, casually frowning at me as if I'd asked him where he'd last seen the house keys.

"I don't see why you're making all this fuss, you can always make more friends," he replied, "but then again, I can't imagine you being that popular."

My eyebrows shot up towards my hairline, my jaw dropping but my mind empty of any reply. I couldn't wrap my head around what he'd said. 'Make more friends' as if Elle was disposable like a broken toy or a soulless vessel that I could just replace.

"Where is she?" I asked.

"I sent her on an errand. I promised I'd let her go once she finished," Louis replied.

"Can't you do it yourself?" I asked.

"No, it can only be conducted by the living," he stated.

"What errand, then?"

"I need to know how they died."

I frowned, shaking my head as it filled with confusion. "What?" I asked.

Louis sighed, rolling his eyes in an open boredom.

"This house, it won't let us leave," he said, "which wouldn't bother me. It's just I'm stuck here with the others."

His gaze sharpened again, his jaw tightening at the apparent thought of them.

"I want them gone, so they stop upsetting Eva," he said.

I paused, waiting as he softened his posture with a long, relaxing sigh.

"Why can't you remember?" I asked, "I'm no expert, but I hear dying is a hard thing to just... forget."

Louis raised his eyebrow, his face loosening as he released an unimpressed huff.

"No one remembers, that's what keeps us here," he replied, "there are three more. You met my father, then there's the one by the gate, and then my pathetic old mother. Once we have closure, we have a chance to leave."

"So, what do I have to do then?" I asked.

"We are currently tied to the house, but once we find out the truth, our spirits will attach to an object instead," he explained, "if a living person carries that object past the front gate, they'll carry them into the world of the living."

"How can you be sure?" I asked.

"This house is old. There were others before us and that's how they left," he said, "they lured people here before using them."

I frowned, her eyes falling to the floor as a new thought rushed into my head.

"Eva never mentioned any of this," I said.

"I don't see why she would," Louis replied, giving a shrug, "I love my sister, but she's not the brightest."

"But you didn't lure us here, she did," I replied, my voice firming, "if she wanted us to help, she would've said so. Why was she so desperate for us to stay if us leaving would mean—"

I glanced up from the floor, my words halting in my mouth. Louis glared at me as if he were a tiger standing over its prey, the look alone locking my body up in a prison of shock and fear. I remained perfectly still, holding my breath until he finally spoke.

"If you don't make them leave, neither do you or your friend," he uttered, filling each word with a sharp venom.

"So, you don't want, um, I mean, need me to find out about you... or Eva?" I asked.

"No, Eva and I are staying," he said, his voice still tight with anger, "this is our place, and it'll be perfect when it's just us."

"Okay," I replied.

He maintained the glare, keeping me dangling in my fear before he released a growling sigh, closing his eyes as if to compose himself before spreading a plastic smile across his face.

"Good," he said, reaching down beneath the piano, "Eva told me your friend did find the truth about a few of us, but then she disappeared, taking the truth with her, but she left the objects she found."

Raising his hand, he lifted a deep green backpack, my heart rushing up into my throat as I recognised the large 'E' sketched into the front pocket. I flinched as he tossed it towards me. My hands clutched onto it, the fabric slightly worn, understandably so, since Elle had used it since kindergarten, but other than that, it was as if it hadn't aged at all since I last saw it.

"She didn't tell Eva anything about how they died?" I asked.

"I don't think so. You'd have to ask her," he replied.

"Okay, but where would Elle disappear to?" I asked, "the house isn't that big and it's not as if she can leave."

Louis shrugged, his eyes gently scanning the room.

"You'd be surprised," he said, "the house is more than just some walls and floorboards. You step into one room and you might step into one version of it or the other. Thankfully, I haven't seen my mother in a while, not that she leaves that bed much either way."

My mind began to rush with panic, glancing through the foyer to the still empty dining room.

"Take as long as you need. We all have endless time," Louis said.

He turned to properly sit on the stool once more, lifting the cover from the piano before restarting his song. I stood there, my thoughts consuming me. I'd only been inside for a few minutes, but how was that translating to the outside? Had it been hours? Days? Months? Every second I wasted, I could be wasting years of whatever life I had left.

As if reading my thoughts, Louis spoke once again, a strange glee to his voice to contrast the deep tune he plucked from the keyboard.

"The previous owner managed to lure a mother and her baby up here once. By the time they freed him and themselves, the baby was an old woman and the mother... that was a fascinating scream."

I felt my stomach roll, my throat stiffening as Louis gazed up at me with a wet grin. I glared down at him, my disgust quickly giving way to urge as he chuckled before switching to a lighter song. I shivered, hugging Elle's backpack to my chest before I stepped from the room.

I shivered, my hand raking through my short hair as I tried to process it all. Almost on autopilot, I wandered towards the staircase, sitting down before giving my head a light shake. I dug into Elle's backpack, her books and pencil case were gone, leaving it empty except for a few objects. Elle had managed to find two of them, a white feather and a shiny bronze pin with what looked to be a family crest engraved into it. I sighed, letting the self-doubt sink onto me like a heavy blanket. I had an idea of where to start, but everything within me fought to change my mind.

Tucking Elle's smaller backpack into my own, I began to climb the stairs, each step sending a cold chill shooting up my spine. As I reached the top of the stairs, I forced my eyes to land on the door to Mrs. Mortimer's room, actively avoiding Eva's room and the room at the end of the hallway. I don't know why, but I knocked before letting myself inside, poking my head into the candlelit room. Mrs. Mortimer was no longer in bed, but at her dressing table, trying on different hairpins. Her lips were still as blue as a lizard's tongue with her eyes loose in their sockets. She was a small woman, just under five-foot-two, her long, greasy blonde hair just passing her hips. I froze as she caught my reflection in the mirror, pausing before turning around to meet my gaze.

"Well, what do you want?" she asked, "can't you see I'm busy?"

I couldn't even open my mouth to attempt a reply, my mind racing back to the last time I had seen her, screaming at me before I'd bolted from her bedroom.

"What is that on your face?" she asked, her face crinkling as if she'd been hit by a bad smell.

"Er, um, glasses," I replied.

"Yes, I can see that but why are they there?" she scoffed, "as if your scar wasn't enough, now you're insisting on making yourselves even more unpresentable? Between you, your brother and your father, this whole family is a disgrace."

My face creased as confusion swarmed any anger I could've mustered. I shook my head, tearing myself from my cloud of emotions before I glanced around the room. There must've been something in here, anything that Elle latched onto to find the answer. Then again, she's always been smarter than me. I reached into my backpack, pulling out the pin and feather before turning back to Mrs. Mortimer.

"Do you know what these are?" I asked, holding them out for her to see.

"As if I'd ever wear a pin like that, it's hideous," she muttered, "you haven't been playing with the cushions or anything, have you? Why do you have a feather?"

I gave a light shrug before tucking the pin back into my bag, my eyebrow lifting as an idea sparked inside my head. Mrs Mortimer huffed before turning back to the mirror, running her fingers down her blonde hair before reaching for the brush, holding it out to her side whilst facing the mirror.

"Whilst you're here, Eva, you might as well brush my hair," she said.

I ignored her, running my hand along the mattress to ensure that it was indeed flat before sitting down. I froze as the room dipped into blackness, my body falling limp like a doll as I collapsed against the bed. I tried to scream, yet my mouth only slightly parted, my body locked in a coffin-ready position. As soon as it darkened, a golden glow engulfed the room, covering every surface in a thick layer before fading slightly. I laid in the bed, unable to move as I strained my eyes to look around, the bedroom door wide open with a curtained figure standing in the hallway.

A gasp lodged in my throat as my body began to move, my back lifting from the mattress as I sat up. Straining my eyes downwards, I found my hands covered in wrinkles, my short hair now reaching my waist and my button-up shirt replaced with a white nightgown.

"It's late, what do you want?" I snapped at the figure.

If I'd been able to move my jaw, it would have dropped. Louis stepped from the darkness of the hallway, almost unrecognisable thanks to the natural deep blue of his eyes and the blushing peachiness of his skin. He looked so ordinary, like any awkward boy you'd find in any neighbourhood. Yet, even without the purple markings on his neck and death clouding his eyes, he seemed to breathe a black toxicity that sent shivers down my spine, making me feel like a cornered mouse.

"Why do you hate us so much, Mother?" he asked, "what did Eva, what did I, ever do to you?"

Mrs. Mortimer obviously didn't share my fear. She simply scoffed, shifting her body to lie us back down on the bed.

"You're so dramatic," she muttered, "I'm sleeping and you should be too."

"Don't ignore me!" Louis barked, "I'm not Father, when I ask you something, you actually answer me!"

Mrs. Mortimer shot up, my head reeling as she did. Louis now stood over us, his eyes widened as his chest heaved. She squinted at him as he seethed, his rage obvious to me even as I watched from behind his mother's eyes. I'd probably given my own mother that look a thousand times, one of frustration and desperation. My face was tense but my eyes bulged, as if they were about to explode. Mrs. Mortimer chuckled before her tone darkened.

"You were born, that's what you did," she said, "you were never meant to be here in the first place. Because of you, I had to marry that despicable man just so I wouldn't end up on the streets. If I wasn't so good to you, I would have left you and that scar-faced brat long ago."

"Don't call my sister that!" Louis snapped.

Fear rushed through me as Louis took another step towards the bed, his neck bent to stare down at his mother as she laughed in his face once again.

"That's funny coming from you," she said, "when you were little, you hated her. You asked me a thousand times to send her to the pound like a dog."

My back hit the mattress hard, my waist pinned down as a pair of hands locked around my throat. Despite her age, Mrs. Mortimer was still a small, frail woman. No matter how hard she clawed at her son's arms, she still could not haul the slightly taller child off of her. I felt everything she did, the fear pulsing through her veins, the tears tinting her vision and the press around her neck. My lungs burned as I gawked up at Louis, his eyes wide as he kneeled over his mother, his hands firm and purposeful as he continued to strangle her.

Mrs. Mortimer managed a few quiet, croaky gasps as her eyes darted around the room, her feet digging at the mattress as her hands tore at the pillows, sending the goose feathers inside spilling across the bed like blood from a vein. Her eyes landed on the hallway as another figure emerged from the darkness.

"...h-help..." Mrs. Mortimer croaked.

Eva didn't move, standing like a ghost in the door frame, her eyes fixated on Louis as he twisted around to glance at her. I tried to move Mrs. Mortimer's mouth to scream, my head spinning as my body began to shut down.

"Eva, come here," Louis said, his teeth glistening in the candlelight as he grinned.

Eva obeyed, drifting across the room, before standing next to the bed, her eyes wide and glassy as she stared down at her mother who continued to squirm against Louis' hold.

"Tell her about your day, your dolls, whatever you want," he said, his voice growing thin as he began to pant, "she'll listen now, she won't ever ignore us again."

A scream finally left my throat as the darkness consumed me. I leapt from the bed before crashing against the floor. I crawled back into the corner of the room, my shirt soaked in sweat and my chest burning as my heart raced. I felt as if a giant hand was encasing me in its palm, like the house was closing in around me, wrapping chains around my ankles, wrists and throat before feeding on my beating heart.

My vision started to clear as I felt a light touch against my knuckles. I flinched before I glanced down to the floor beside me, finding the once-white feather now dipped in a bright, blood red. My backpack was laid by my feet. With trembling fingers, I drew back the zip, tucking the feather inside with shaky breath. I put my hand over my heart, drawing long soothing breaths as I tried to calm myself.

"What are you doing?"

I yelped, glancing towards the dressing table to see Mrs. Mortimer fully turned around in her seat, her blue lips twisted into an impatient sneer.

"I told you to come and brush my hair!" she snapped.

"Shut up, you fucking bitch! If you hate me so much, if I'm such a fucking burden to you, why didn't you just drop me off at Dad's and never come back? Why put up with me? Why force me to put up with you?" I screamed, "I'm not the fucking daughter you wanted, okay? Get over it and leave me alone!"

Tears rolled down my cheeks as my words tore up my throat like pieces of rough sandpaper. Mrs. Mortimer gazed back at me, frowning with widened eyes. I brought my legs to my chest, burying my face into my knees as I shuddered out several deep sobs. I rocked myself back and forth as I let my emotions wash over me like a cold shower, stuttering them out between snuffles.

"How did you do that?"

The sound of that voice sent an electric shock through my body. I jolted, my back slapping against the wall as I gazed up at her. Eva was exactly how I'd last seen her, not so much as a hair out of place with her whitened eyes still fixated on me. I sat in silence, stuck in a cloud of shock before I finally forced the words out.

"Do what?" I asked.

"Talk to her like that and get away with it," she replied.

"I don't know, I wasn't even talking to her really."

"Oh, I'm sorry," she replied.

"What do you mean 'sorry?'" I asked, wrinkling my nose.

"Whoever you were talking to," she replied, "they must not be very nice."

My face twisted into a deep scowl as I glared up at her, a rush of bitterness flushing through me.

"Speaking of which, why are you being so nice?" I muttered.

Eva's eyes fell to the floor, her fingers tugging at the rims of her sleeves. Wiping another layer of tears from my cheek, I glanced towards hers, they were still purple and vivid against her bluish skin. For some reason, I assumed her scar was similar to the markings on Louis' neck, or the blood running down her father's face— that it was a consequence of death. She'd received it when she was alive; it hadn't killed her.

Glancing back up from the floor, she finally mumbled.

"I just wanted to play. I didn't want to hurt anyone."

I felt myself soften at that, my jaw tensing as I tried to block out any sympathy I felt for her. Yet, I couldn't bear the weight of her innocent face staring back at me with wide puppy-dog eyes. I sighed, pushing myself from the floor with my backpack in hand.

"Are you going to help me or not?" I asked.

"I'm not sure if Louis would like that," she replied, swallowing down, "but maybe for a little while..."

I gave her a slight nod, pulling my backpack over my shoulders.

"Do you know where Elle is, then?" I asked.

She shook her head. I ran my hand through my now-sweaty head of hair before reaching to take my glasses from my nose, using the fabric of my shirt to clean them.

"I've never seen a girl with short hair," Eva remarked.

"Yeah, I do it myself because my parents won't let me go to the hairdressers'," I mumbled, making my way towards the stairs, "you should've seen their faces the next morning, you'd think I'd killed a puppy or something."

Eva let out a short chuckle as she followed me downstairs, counting the steps as we descended.

"Could you cut mine one day?" she asked, "mine has been so long for forever."

I glanced over my shoulder to watch as she toyed with her long locks. Why was I even talking to her like that? Like I was talking to a little cousin? No matter how hard I tried to slap myself with the truth, I kept seeing a little girl staring back at me from behind those dead eyes. I brushed off a chill before he reached the bottom of the stairs.

"Sure, maybe," I mumbled. "so, do your parents know they're...you know?"

"Dead?" Eva replied, "that they're dead?"

A felt a lump swell in my throat, the casualness of how she said it making my skin crawl. It was like she was talking about jam or the weather, so matter-of-fact to the point of an unnerving unconcern. I nodded, watching as she sat down on the staircase, her eyes gazing off into the corner of the foyer.

"I didn't know for a long time. I just didn't think about it. I never wondered why I never got any taller, why I looked so pale, why I never ate anything. When Louis figured it out, I didn't want to hear about it, neither did Mother or Father. It was scary to talk about it, like I was talking about someone else. It couldn't be me—I couldn't be dead."

Silence filled the space between us as she continued to stare ahead as if trying to absorb what she'd just said. I adjusted my glasses before clearing my throat, the silence too full and overbearing for me.

"Louis said there were others that... died before you," I said, "is there anyone else, you know, wandering around?"

"They've all managed to leave," Eva replied.

"Then who's the other one in the yard?" I asked, "Louis wanted me to get rid of them. Do you have any other brothers or sisters?"

"No," Eva replied, shaking her head, "Louis won't let me near them and they never come into the house, so I don't know who they are."

I sighed before crossing the foyer towards the door, giving it a hard pull. It refused to budge. I glanced back to Eva as she remained on the staircase.

"How do you open this?" I asked.

"Um, well, it's unlocked normally, but sometimes it locks," she replied.

"Why?" I asked.

Eva glanced down towards her feet, pressing her knees together and hunching her shoulders.

"Because we can lock it," she replied, "I just have to focus on it."

"Can you open it for me then?" I replied, letting out a breath of frustration.

Eva just stared at me, lightly tapping her heels against the stairs.

"We can play dolls instead, or tea party," she murmured, "I still have some of Elle's books."

I fought back a glare, anger bubbling in my chest. I glanced down to the door and then back towards Eva, taking in a deep breath.

"You can come with me," I said, holding out my hand, "here, it's okay."

I tried to soften my face as she glanced back at me, staring at my hand as if it held a grenade. She rose to her feet, stepping across the foyer, glancing into the living room to find it, and the piano, unoccupied. Eva turned back towards me, her shoulders hunched and her eyes locked on my hand before she finally stepped forward, her small fingers encasing my own. I flinched, having never directly touched her before. She was so cold. I felt as if someone had draped a chilled rag across my palm, chills rippling up my spine as I gripped her hand. There was a faint click behind me, my eyes landing on the door. A spark of relief flushed through me as I reached for the door, pushing it open with a light tap.

"It's been a little while," Eva murmured.

My lips parted as I read the genuine nervousness that spread across her face, her lips tilted into a slight frown and her eyes narrowed. I gave her hand a light squeeze, forcing a small smile before we stepped out onto the porch. To my discomfort, night had turned to day. Rainclouds swarmed the sky, sending tiny drops of water falling to the yellow grass beneath and a cool breeze running through the woods.

"At least the grass will get some water," I murmured, trying to ignore the question of how long I'd been cooped up inside.

"It never helps," Eva mumbled, "it always stays this colour, no matter how much it rains."

"How do you know?" I asked, "the curtains are always closed."

"We can move those too," she replied, "it's our house after all."

I sighed, anxiety fizzling inside my head as I scanned the dying garden, my mind empty of any ideas. Still holding Eva's hand, I reached into the backpack to pull out the pin, holding it in my open palm.

"Do you know what this is?" I asked.

Eva squinted at it, tilting her head as a spark of recognition flashed across her eyes.

"I think I've seen it before," she said.

I glanced back up to the garden, raking my eyes over the dead, leafless bushes and dug up garden beds. I needed the spot where they died, whoever they were. Eva followed my gaze, her eyes sharpening as she lifted a single finger towards the wooden skeleton of a long-dead rose bush.

"Try there," she said.

I took in a deep breath before kneeling on the spot, gently releasing my grip from Eva's hand as she hovered over me. My muscles tightened as I pressed my hand against the grass, feeling the warmth of the dirt before glancing back to Eva who gave me a shrug.

"Why here?" I asked, continuing to run my hand over the grass, spreading out further to the left.

"I don't know, I just feels familiar—"

I froze in place as a pair of dirt-covered shoes brushed against my fingertips. My stomach rolled up into my throat as I remained on all fours, my arms trembling beneath my weight.

"Why?"

I swallowed hard as I glanced up, following a dusty pair of trousers until I found the ghostly figure's face. It was youthful and soft, baby fat still clinging to his blood-stained cheeks. His eyes and their sockets were a pitch-black, his head titled as he gazed down at Eva. I twisted my head to gawk back at Eva, her eyes wide and her form trembling as she stared up at him.

"...why am I still here?" he stuttered.

I leapt back, only for the darkness to grip me once again, swarming me like hungry leeches to carrion. Then the gold layer came, engulfing the dark to build a new scenery. My heart raced inside my chest as I fell into the new body, a sour nausea filling my mouth and my limbs stiffening.

I stood on the porch looking over the garden that was littered with fresh flower beds blooming with white roses and lavender bushes. The grass was a vibrant green and the sky a salmon pink as the orange sun set behind the trees. Despite the glow of the garden, I felt a heavy helplessness, unable to control the body I inhabited, unable to change the inevitable.

I caught a morphed reflection of myself in the darkened window. My skin crawled as I glimpsed the male body I was stuck in. The boy was slightly younger than Louis, with reddish hair and freckles. He wore a dark brown suit that scratched against his skin and a sparkling gold pin against his beige tie.

"Are you coming?"

The boy glanced from his reflection, finding Louis and Eva standing at the bottom of the porch stairs. He followed them into the garden, straightening his back to try and stand as tall as Louis.

"Did you like my singing?" Eva asked, a slight smile sitting on top of her chin.

The boy glanced down at Eva. Her hair was neatly brushed and styled so that most of her scar was hidden beneath her fringe, she wore a white dress with a pink bow around the waist. I couldn't help but shiver every time I saw her alive, the image of her ghostly figure looming behind her blushing, breathing face.

"It was all right," the boy replied "I liked the piano better though."

The boy glanced over to Louis, only to be met with a side-eyed glare. The boy didn't seem bothered though, keeping the gaze for a few seconds before turning back to Eva.

"Why must you live all the way out here?" he asked, "we had to travel for hours, and that pathetic little village down the hill is disgusting."

"Father inherited it," Louis replied, his voice hard as stone.

"Your father's a fool," the boy chuckled, "you're lucky my father associates with him at all, given our stature."

The boy glanced down at his tie to jab at the shiny pin that glowed against the softened light. Out of the corner of the boy's eye, I saw Louis' slight sneer melt away into a slick smirk.

"Do you even know how to spell half those words, Clifford?" Louis huffed, a sinister mischief sparking in his tone, "you should pin that thing to your forehead if you're so proud of it."

Clifford's eyes snapped towards Louis before they darted towards Eva, his hand lashing out to grab hers. Eva frowned, glancing between Clifford and Louis with mouse-like eyes.

"So, my father says he's thinking of marrying us," Clifford said, "it wouldn't be too bad, your face isn't too unsightly, and we could tear down the house and sell the land."

Eva blinked up at him, almost as if, for a brief minute, she liked that idea before fear washed over her face. She squeaked as Louis gripped her arm, yanking her back as he took a step towards Clifford. My heart began to pound as Louis' glare darkened, yet remained still and calm. He was unpredictable, like a grenade. I could see Clifford's reflection in Louis' eyes, a wicked smirk plastered across his face as he enjoyed Louis' reaction.

"You'd have to get through me," Louis growled.

Clifford chuckled, shaking his head in his glee.

"Come on, I'm doing you all a favour," he said, "who else would want that ugly thing... or even that house at the very least?"

Clifford opened his mouth to release another laugh, only for the air to burst from his lungs as Louis sprang. I tried to scream, but Clifford's mouth was smothered by Louis' hand, his throat blocked by the bend of Louis' knee. Dread mixed with my panic, burning through me with Clifford's fear. No, not again.

"I'll show you ugly," Louis spat.

Clifford wheezed and gasped for air as Louis reached for Clifford's necktie, tearing off the pin with a sharp rip. From the corner of Clifford's eyes, I could see Eva, her hands clasped over her mouth as she glanced between Clifford and the house, edging towards the porch.

"Louis, no!" Eva gasped, "stop it. Father will hear you!"

"Only if you don't shut up!" Louis snapped.

Clifford tried to cry out, yet only a pathetic wheeze eased from his compressed throat. His hands clawed at Louis' leg, his body twisting to try and shove Louis off of him. Louis' eyes sparked, a grin spreading across his face as he popped the needle of the pin from its holder, the sharp tip glinting in the fading light.

"Maybe not on your forehead," Louis muttered.

His smile grew as he pressed the pin forward, the needle piercing Clifford's eyeball as if it were a softened grape. My body seared with pain, my screams collecting in my throat as Clifford continued to thrash, tears and blood falling from his eyes. Louis grunted, rocking forward to apply his full weight onto Clifford's neck, a rough crunch snapping through Clifford's tight gasps.

Clifford went limp, his arms and legs flopping like the tentacles of a beached squid. The vision in his remaining eye began to blur as blood rolled down his opposite cheek. With a low grunt, Louis pushed himself off of Clifford's neck. My heart rammed inside my chest, desperate for Clifford to move, to defy his paralysed body. Yet, he laid there like a discarded doll, the pin still wedged into his eye socket.

Louis raised his feet, stumbling slightly as he turned to face Eva, who stood frozen in place, her jaw unlocked and her eyes fixated on Clifford. Louis panted as he staggered towards her, clapping her cheeks with his blood-stained hands.

"I'm a good brother, aren't I?" he asked, his voice thin and shivering, "tell me!"

Eva tucked her chin down into her chest, her eyes squeezed shut as Louis' words passed through her like a gush of wind.

"...Yes," she replied.

Louis' breath slowed, his face softening as he loosened his grip on Eva's arms.

"No one will ever take you away from this place or from me," he said, "I promise."

Eva didn't respond, keeping her eyes fixated on the ground, her body locked up.

"And you are beautiful," Louis replied.

Clifford wheezed, prompting Louis and Eva to snap back towards him, their eyes widened. Louis removed his hands from Eva's face, leaving two bloodied handprints on her ghostly cheeks. He stumbled towards Clifford, stepping out of my field of vision before I felt a pair of hands latch onto Clifford's ankles, dragging his body towards the gate.

"Go," Louis grunted, tugging the body further, "if they ask, tell them he ran off somewhere. I'll take care of it."

The shadows around me began to grow, swelling into a familiar darkness as Clifford's eyes began to droop shut, a final tear falling from his lashes. Life rushed back to me, allowing a scream to fall from my lips as I jolted from the grass, clumps of dirt flying from beneath my kicking heels. My throat swelled as a fresh coat of sweat covered my body, falling into my burning eyes. I collapsed, trying to slow my breaths and the rapid pace of my heart. Despite the cool relief that washed through me, I didn't want to move. The weight of the two deaths clung to me like a heavy backpack, keeping me pinned to the ground.

I heard a slight shuffle from above, my neck straining as I forced myself to look up. There he was, staring down at me with blackened eyes and a slight frown. I curled inwards from where I lay, a spark of fear igniting within me from amongst the grey numbness.

"I want to go home," he wheezed.

Time must have done wonders for his arrogance. His eyes welled with tears, his arms loose at his sides. I felt a strange urge to hold him, but my fear kept me glued to the ground.

"I'll take you home," I replied, "just in a little while, wait here."

"Okay," he mumbled.

I watched as he turned, wandering through the garden and towards the gate. There he sank to sit, crossing his legs before staring down the path to the bottom of the hill. He seemed so small in comparison to the tall, imprisoning fence. I pushed aside the wave of pity before climbing to my feet, running my fingers through my hair before I spotted Eva. She stared at Clifford, her face softened with a slight frown.

"Do you want to leave too?" I asked.

"I don't know. I've never been anywhere else," she mumbled, turning her gaze to the forest, "people always look at me funny because of my face...and it's scary out there. It's so big and noisy."

I took in a quiet breath as I stared down at her, sucking in my lips before I convinced myself to say something.

"There's nothing wrong with your face," I said, "if people don't like it, that's their problem not yours, okay?"

Eva blinked up at me, her forehead creasing before she bowed her head, turning to wander back towards the house, slipping inside without another sound. I adjusted my glasses before I scanned the ground beneath me, finding the pin now laying amongst the yellow grass, coated in red.

Kneeling down, I placed the pin into my backpack, watching as it settled next to the feather before returning to the house. Despite its limited contents, the backpack seemed so heavy, the straps digging into my shoulders. I carried the weight up the porch stairs, the images of Louis standing over me, or rather Mrs. Mortimer and Clifford, flashed before my eyes, sending a chill trickling down my spine. I gripped onto the door handle, nausea rising within me as I tried to force back the flashing scenes painted across my eyes.

My hot breath burned my throat and lungs as I tried to calm my shuddering body, my mind falling back to the iron gates behind me. I could run. I could leave now and never have to think about this again. I stiffened, refusing to move and give into the temptation, letting out a frustrated growl before pushing back inside the house.

As I slipped into the foyer, I peeked into the living room to find the table full of food once again. My eyes lit up as I took another step to peek through the door frame. Eva and Louis' father, or rather, Mr. Mortimer, sat at the head of his table, overlooking the food before him with his loosely clenched fist resting against his nose and lips. I felt his eyes land on me as I stepped into the room, trying to find the window as I traced the floor around the table.

"Don't even think about helping yourself, these are for my guests only, important gentlemen," he muttered, referring to the food "I'm sure you've never even seen food like this; you're probably from the village."

I glanced up from the table and towards him, a tang of pity filling my chest. How long had he been sitting at that table waiting for guests to arrive? Had he ever wondered why the curtains were always drawn? Why the food never got cold? How many years had he been trapped in the delusion that he was alive?

"Look, this may be hard to think about but... you are dead, okay? So—"

"What are you talking about?" he said, his eyes darting across the table as if trying to avoid the truth, "you're as mad as that other girl. Did they build some kind of asylum nearby that I wasn't notified of? Is that why so many crazy people come wandering through my house?"

"If there were an asylum, I bet your son would be in it," I spat.

Mr. Mortimer sank back in his seat, his eyes freezing over. He blinked furiously as if his mind was performing gymnastics inside his skull. He glanced up to me, a slight desperation painting his blank expression.

"Are you here to evaluate him?" he asked, "is this some kind of... act, so he won't catch on? Are you one of those new women doctors or something?"

I squinted at him, tilting my head before I decided to jump at it.

"Y-yes, sir," I asked, faking an affirming smile.

"So, I can get rid of him?" he asked, straightening his posture, "how much will it cost? Is it just treatment or is it boarding as well? Why am I even bothering asking you? I want to speak to your supervisor."

"I have some questions first," I replied.

I began to circle the room again, trying to slip into the right place. I felt Mr. Mortimer's stare follow me. I cleared my throat before summoning a question.

"So, um, your wife told me he wasn't... planned," I said.

"She told you that? I thought she'd carry it to the grave," Mr. Mortimer replied, raising his eyebrow, "it was her own fault really, not mine, that she got pregnant."

I sucked my lips inward, fighting back a smart-ass response as I continued to circle the room. Another thought made its way to the front of my mind, Eva's pale face flashing before my eyes.

"How did Eva get that scar on her face?" I asked.

Mr. Mortimer's eyes fell to the table, his bloodied lips parting before he reached up to cup his hand over his mouth with a long sigh.

"This is confidential, yes?" he asked, his voice deepening as he swallowed down.

"Yes," I replied, stopping in my tracks to stand beside his chair.

"My wife originally wanted a girl so she was happier to deal with Eva over Louis," he explained, shifting in his seat as he avoided eye contact with me, "one day, Louis was ten, Eva was... six? We had some acquaintances over, family friends, you know... After a little while we noticed the children were gone. We went outside and they'd been playing football in the garden. Not a problem, but my wife was furious because Eva had gotten all filthy playing with the boys so she took her inside to clean up. Louis...didn't like that."

"How do you know?" I asked.

"Well he threw a fit of course, but he went all quiet when my wife told Eva she was to stay inside and have afternoon tea with the ladies," he replied, "I should have known. He only acts up when he thinks he doesn't have control. When he's sure of himself, he goes all quiet."

"So, he was jealous of Eva?" I asked, squinting down at him.

"I think so, for a while at least. It's not uncommon with siblings after all, but..." Mr. Mortimer responded, his mouth remaining open before he finally found the words, "this is what my wife told me. Right after she got cleaned up, Eva, my wife and a few of her friends were having afternoon tea. The ladies loved her; she was as cute as a doll and my wife loved showing her off."

The fear I found in Mr. Mortimer's eyes was the first non-superficial thing he had shown me. He stared off into the corner of the room, resting the knuckle of his forefinger against his lips, his face worn and old as he recalled the events.

"And then, um, Louis comes in and says that he wants to tell Eva a secret," he said, his voice trailing into a loose mumble, "my wife told him to hurry up, so he stepped towards Eva and asked her to lean in so he could tell her."

My heart started ramming in my chest, my eyes following Mr. Mortimer's hand as he reached for his wine, taking a quick swig from the glass. He muffled a strong cough before staring back down at the table.

"Next thing we knew, Eva started to scream. That's when I ran in and there's blood everywhere, the carpet, the table cloth, everything. It was disgusting," he said, his face creasing, "Louis had taken a knife from the kitchen and thought it would be...interesting to slice her cheek open."

"W-why?"

"Everyone asked him that, you'd think he'd have a good answer, even for a ten-year-old," he replied, his jaw tightening, "but he always just smiled as if he was smarter than everyone else. He did it more often when he realised that it set people off."

My shoulders hunched, a slight nausea running up my throat. Mr. Mortimer shook his head, clearing his throat as he snapped from his bitter trance.

"After that, my wife might as well have disowned Eva. She didn't brush her hair or take her dress shopping like she used to. She asked me to try for another baby, but stopped pushing for it when I asked what would happen if we had another boy," he said.

"What about Louis?" I asked.

"That's what makes no bloody sense. He stabs the girl in the face and then suddenly he loves her more than the sun and the sky," he replied.

"Maybe he felt guilty?" I asked, earning harsh scoff from Mr. Mortimer.

"There is not one ounce of guilt in that boy's body," he huffed, "in fact, she apologised to him."

"What for?" I asked, knitting my brows.

Mr. Mortimer shrugged.

"Well, rationally, I asked her what she'd done to provoke him and she didn't know. So, after they stitched her up, she told him she was sorry," he replied, "he never left her alone after that. Not that she wanted him to, she started clinging to him like fish to water."

"How horrible," I mumbled.

"I know! No one would associate with me anymore. I was the joke with the disturbed children!" Mr. Mortimer spat.

I couldn't keep the disgusted scowl from my face, my nose scrunching and my mouth easing open as Mr. Mortimer took another sip of wine, another cough rumbling up his throat. I ran my eyes over the table and his precious banquet before I focused on his chair, positioned at the head of the table with the powerful fire behind him.

"Hey, I think you have a stain on your shoes," I said.

Mr. Mortimer shot from the chair, stepping away from the table to examine his shiny black dress shoes, his face creasing as he found them untouched.

"What are you talk—"

I shoved myself into the seat, gold encasing me once again. A rush of panic seized me, my body shivering against the chair as I realised what I had to go through once again. The room remained the same except for an orange glow that filled it. I glanced out of the window to see the blooming sunset over the black of the trees. In front of me, sat a small roast dinner, along with Eva and Louis.

Louis scratched his knife and fork against his plate as he cut up his vegetables, making me cringe at the sharp, grating sound. Eva sat in complete silence, her plate empty and her hands resting in her lap. Mr. Mortimer took over, reaching a hand out to take a sip of wine from his glass, his eyes darting between his two children.

"They still haven't found poor Clifford's body, thank you for your concern," he muttered, huffing once he was met with silence, "you know, you two seem to be only good at one thing and that's setting this family back."

Eva shivered in her seat whilst Louis dabbed his mouth with a napkin.

"You've got to be joking," he replied, still chewing on a piece of meat, "we were doing fine in the city. You dragged us out here because you wanted a big fancy house to make yourself feel important for once."

I jolted as Mr. Mortimer's fist slammed the table in front of me, prompting the surface to tremble and clatter beneath his anger.

"We moved out here so that you two could be as far away from people as possible!" Mr. Mortimer snapped.

"Then you have no one to blame but yourself," Louis replied, "you shouldn't've let us wander off with him then."

Mr. Mortimer clenched his fists, his knuckles turning a chalky white as he turned towards his daughter, whose eyes were still fixated on her lap.

"Nothing to say, Eva?" he spat, "not hungry?"

Mr. Mortimer rose from his seat, tracing the tabletop with a finger until he reached Eva's seat. In the seat beside her, sat one of her dolls, as if she'd invited a friend to dinner. She reached under the arm of her own chair to hold the doll's hand, squeezing tightly as her father hovered over her, gripping the back of Eva's chair and bending down to cast his dark shadow over her.

"What did he do to him?" he asked, "and where did he put him?"

"She doesn't know," Louis replied, his voice firming, "and neither will you. I doubt you'll want to know, actually."

"You don't get to tell me what I want and what I don't want," Mr. Mortimer raged, "I have his bloody father and the police breathing down my neck."

"You'll have a lot more people breathing down your neck if they find him," Louis replied with a sparkling chuckle, "but then again, it's been a few months and I doubt any animal would let fresh meat go to waste. So, no need to worry, Father dear."

"You're revolting!" Mr. Mortimer spat.

Mr. Mortimer's eyes trailed back down to Eva, locking onto the doll.

"You're ten years old, you should be done with dolls by now!" he snapped.

His hand shot towards the doll, tugging it from its chair. Eva kept her grip, her eyes widening in a flash of panic as he glared down at her. He tried to tug it away from her, only for her to yank it back towards her. I tensed as I saw a slight shift in her face, her soft expression hardening as she lowered her eyebrows, her eyes filling with a familiar darkness. Mr. Mortimer leaned towards her.

"You little—"

Mr. Mortimer gagged, his mouth hanging open as his eyes fixated on Eva. Panic sparked within me as I couldn't see what'd happened until Eva pulled back, slowly dragging the steak knife with her. The blade shone with red, sending a shower of blood to sprinkle across her cheeks and over the table, the food soaking up each cursed drop as Mr. Mortimer stumbled backwards, clasping his hand over the gaping hole in his throat.

"What did you do that for?" Louis hissed, "he's our bank!"

Eva didn't reply as Mr. Mortimer fell back into his seat, bracing himself against the table as blood poured from his neck and mouth like wine flowing from a broken bottle. Eva kept her eyes on him, her face sunken and her lips tilted into a slight frown as she held the doll close to her chest with one hand and the bloody knife in the other.

"I wanted to see if I could do it," she mumbled, allowing the steak knife to slip from her grip. It fell with a clatter.

Mr. Mortimer slumped forward, his cheek pressed against the table, sending a coating of blood over its surface before the blackness consumed him. I gasped, my body jolting as I fell from the chair, slapping hard against the floor as my eyes darted around the room.

"What is wrong with you?" Mr. Mortimer barked, reaching to lift the toppled chair from the floor, "you really are crazy!"

I froze as I glanced down the table, finding Eva standing by her seat, staring down at me with interest.

"Did Louis kill him too?" she asked.

I trembled like an alarm clock, fear pulsing through me. I couldn't do it anymore. I had to run. I had to get out of there. I glanced behind her, finding the steak knife where she'd dropped it, still coated in red. My body trembled as I forced myself to stand, my knees jerking as I lunged forward, snatching the knife before charging into the foyer. I skidded to a halt as I found Louis at the piano, glancing over his shoulder at me as he continued to play.

"You look horrible—what's the matter?" he asked, in a chiming yet mocking tone.

A cocktail of rage and horror surged through me, my body prickling with nerves.

"You fucking monster!" I screamed.

I didn't wait for his reply, lunging for the staircase. I went for the first door I saw, stumbling into Eva's room, collapsing against the door, slamming it shut against my back. I covered my face with my palms, gritting my teeth. I still couldn't cry, my chest twisted like a tight rag. I don't know how long I stayed in that room, counting each straining heartbeat until my breath slowed. I rested my chin against my knees, soaking in the precious silence.

I froze as I heard a slight shuffle against the floorboards, my eyes zipping across the room. I held my breath, waiting for another noise.

"Eva?" I called.

No one replied as my eyes landed on the bed. I reached into my backpack, discarding the steak knife and replacing it with the larger one I had brought. Sliding on my knees, I approached the bed, pausing before I lowered my cheek to the floor. I recoiled as a pair of bloodshot eyes gaped back at me, the red veins reaching out to lick the dark irises. The figure crouched by the head of the bed, coiled up like a snake with its arm and legs tucked in. A shivering breath exited my throat, my lips tilting into a saddened smile.

"Elle?" I whispered.

She didn't reply, gaping back at me whilst keeping as still as a rabbit ready to pounce. A bittersweet joy rolled through me as I shifted closer to the bed. Elle flinched, her form shifting away from me like a vampire retreating from the morning sun. My glee was quickly soaked in confusion.

"It's me—it's Zoe," I said, my mind racing as her pale face remained unchanged, "I got new glasses."

Elle's stare passed through me, as if I were completely transparent. She blinked as if accepting my existence, tears clotting her eyes as her bottom lip trembled.

"Zoe?" she asked, "w-where were you?"

Guilt pierced my chest, blooming inside me as I pressed my chest against the floor.

"I couldn't find you," I replied, "I'm so sorry I took so long, but we can go home soon, come on."

I reached back beneath the bed, holding out my hand. Elle gawked at it, her head retreating back like a turtle withdrawing into its shell.

"I can't," she whispered, "I tried... but it was too much. I lost the trinkets."

"I found them," I said with a breathless smile.

"Sorry," Elle mumbled, hiding her face in her folded arms.

"No, that's okay," I replied, slipping off my backpack for her to see, "we have them all now, the mother, the father and Clifford's, so we just have to get Louis or Eva to let us out."

My triceps tensed as my desperation bloomed, sucking my lips inward as I waited for her reply.

"I don't want to see them," Elle mumbled, her form trembling with every word spoken, "I asked them to let me go. Louis laughed at me, and Eva wouldn't do anything. I begged them but they wouldn't listen to me. It was like I couldn't speak. Why would they let me go now?"

"It'll be different," I replied, "we can do this and you'll never have to deal with it again."

"You're still so fucking naïve," Elle muttered, her face souring as a tear carved her reddened cheek, "you can't promise that. Don't you ever promise me that!"

I shifted backwards, drawing back my hand. I glanced down at the floor as a beehive of emotions swarmed within me, my bottom lip twitching as frustration overflowed within me. With a deep breath, I reached out my hand again, fully extending it beneath the bed. I waited for Elle to lift her gaze towards me.

"I can promise that I'll be there," I said.

Elle blinked away her tears, her brows arching slightly as she gazed at me, then my open palm. She reached up to dry her soaked cheeks, biting her lip as she took in a slow breath. She emptied her lungs with an equally long breath before she shifted, taking my hand before crawling out from beneath the bed.

She was taller than me, even with her hunched posture. Her once-oversized jumper now reached the middle of her forearm, her jeans cut away to make shorts that were like a second skin against her thighs. Her brown hair brushed her knees. It made me wish I had a hair tie to offer her. She gawked down at me before lifting her hands to gaze at them, now long and slender in comparison to her once short, stumpy child hands.

"How long?" she asked.

I took her hand, encasing it in both of mine before giving it a light squeeze.

"Let's just go home, okay?" I replied.

"Do you really think they'll let us?" she asked.

I opened my mouth to reply, only for my voice to be replaced by the soft tune of a violin. Elle tensed up, locking her sweaty fingers around mine. I picked my backpack up from the ground before leading Elle out into the hallway. I paused outside the door at the end of the hall, the music vibrating from behind the door. I gave Elle a weak smile before reaching to knock on the door. The music stopped, the silence tight and heavy.

"Yes?"

"It's us," I replied.

"Come in, then."

I pushed open the door to reveal an attic-like bedroom with a single bed shoved against the wall with a plain beige bed cover and lumpy pillow. There was a single window at the front of the house with an empty candle holder resting against the windowpane. The walls were tall with rafters separating draped across the arched ceiling. At best, this was an old storage room, making it painfully apparent who the preferred Mortimer child was.

Louis sat in a wooden chair in the corner of the room, violin and bow resting in his rotting fingers.

"You play violin too?" I asked.

"Yes, Father bought it for Eva to try and make her more appealing to suitors, but well..." he replied, focusing on his playing, "can you believe I only started learning post mortem?"

"But why?" I asked, raising a brow.

"Oddly enough, I have a lot of time on my hands," he replied, locking the bow behind his neck before his eyes landed on us. I felt Elle shiver behind me, "so, I assume you have something to tell me?"

I stiffened, straightening my posture before pulling on my backpack. Elle remained stone still beside me, as if moving an inch would provoke him.

"We have them all, you just have to let us out," I replied.

"Perfect," Louis said with a grin, "I'll have to chase those two out myself, but at least that'll be the end of it."

"What about Clifford?" I asked.

"Oh, he knows— that's why he waits by the gate," Louis replied, giving a light chuckle, "little bastard still thinks his father is waiting for him at home."

I glanced at Elle, her face softening with a slight relief.

"Bye, then," I said.

I smiled at Elle as we turned towards the door, my stomach dropping as it slammed shut, meeting Eva's puppy stare instead.

"No..." she said, "you can't go. We can still play."

My mind raced, the first words that came to me falling from my lips.

"You can come with us," I said, "you don't have to stay here."

"I wouldn't push my luck."

My body stiffened as I heard Louis' sharp voice behind me, a chill carving down my spine.

"It's safer here, it's scary out there. Louis can't protect me out there, but you can stay here too, you never have to leave," Eva replied, almost as if rehearsed, "and they can't bother us anymore, so it'll just be us."

I readjusted my grip on Elle's hand as she began to tremble, her widened eyes fixated on me as I swallowed the swelling lump in my throat. I reached into my open backpack, careful not to cut my fingers on the knives before I reached the soft material. I dragged the doll out by its arm, holding it out to Eva with a trembling grip.

"Here," I said.

Eva stared at the doll, her eyes watering before she lashed out a hand, knocking the doll from grip, sending it tumbling into the corner of the room. Elle yelped, her shoulder brushing mine as Eva stomped her foot against the floor.

"No!" she screamed. Together, we stepped back into the centre of the room as the now-familiar gold glaze smothered the room.

"Zoe!" Elle gasped.

I felt Elle's arms lock around me as my stomach twisted into a knot. Fear burst through my chest, my eyes prickling with tears as the dread washed over me. Yet Elle's tight grip pierced through the cold chill that rushed down my body, a slight but warm reassurance flushing through me before my vision cleared.

I saw a pair of small-ish dress shoes and a pair of trousers as Louis' gaze dropped to the wooden chair in which he stood before he glanced back up to the rope he'd slung over the rafters in the ceiling. His fingers began to twist the rope into a wide noose, a lump forming in my throat as I recalled the blood that once stained those fingers.

"What are you doing?"

Louis turned towards the door, found Eva as she stepped into the room, her eyes locked onto him. He paused, his gaze flipping between his sister and the rope.

"Decorating," Louis replied after a short pause, "you need something?"

"Who were those people today?" Eva asked.

Louis paused, squeezing the rope beneath his fingers before continuing.

"I don't know," he replied, "I told them Father was on a hunting trip. They bought it, but I think they'll be back."

"Maybe they won't care," Eva replied.

"Still," Louis mumbled, "could you blow out that candle for me?"

Louis kept his eyes on the knot, listening to Eva's footsteps as she passed him to approach the candle on the window sill. His gaze fell to the floor as he slipped to the floor, my eyes landing on a bulky lump on the leg of his trousers. There was something in his pocket, I only caught a slight glimpse from the corner of Louis' eye but I couldn't let the sharp curiosity leave me. Louis then approached the door, pushing it closed and locking it with a heavy click before tucking the golden key into the front pocket of his jacket.

"Louis, what are you doing?" Eva asked.

Louis ignored her, climbing back onto the chair. He stared through the noose, a lump rising in his throat. My mind raced, my heart lurching inside my chest as he stared at the knot, as if it were another challenge.

"They'll separate us," he stumbled, reaching for the rope to loop it over his head, "they'll take you away."

"Louis, no!"

With a short sigh, he reached for the gun, his finger firm against the trigger as he aimed it at his sister, her face white and her eyes wet and glistening. I froze behind Louis' eyes, unable to decide whether or not he would do it. He'd killed twice before, that I knew of, what was one more? Even if it was Eva?

"Together, yes?" he said, his breath growing thin, "always together."

Louis squeezed the trigger as Eva lunged forward. Suddenly, he was weightless, his feet kicking in the air beneath him before he plunged down, falling into a thick cloud of darkness. I gasped as gold replaced the black, my head reeling as I squinted against the light. I stared down to find a pair of small hands braced against the floor beneath me, breathing heavily as tears dotted the wooden panels. Eva rose to her feet, trembling as she glanced over her shoulder at Louis as he swayed like a willow tree branch in a soft breeze.

Eva sank to the floor, resting against the door as she watched him hang there, tears flowing from her eyes. The sky gradually began to darken, and she tried to open the locked door, tugging at it between sobs. She lit the candle by the window to fight away the dark, tucking herself into the corner of the room. I waited with her as days passed, feeling the turn of her empty stomach and dry tongue.

She eventually gained the courage to approach Louis' body, reaching into his trouser pocket to retrieve the key, unlocking the door. She gradually ate away at the leftover food in the pantry, her body eating away at her flesh as she ran out. She would always return to Louis' room, ignoring the flies that began to hover around his corpse. The thought to leave, to stumble down to the village or the closest town came to her, yet her fear kept her captive. She couldn't survive without him, she convinced herself.

The black slowly began to creep around her, like a predator waiting for its large prey to weaken before striking. Leaning against the wall, her stomach too empty to growl and her limbs too weak to lift her, she gazed at the flickering light of the candle. The wick was worn down to its last millimetre, her eyes desperately clinging to the flickering light before, at last, it distinguished.

"Zoe!"

My feet kicked at the floor, my back slamming against the wall. I felt it again, the house's pull, the urge to sink to the ground and merge with it. I yelped as a pair of hands gripped me, my gaze landing on a pair of soft eyes. I stilled as Elle locked her arms around me, her fingers tracing through my sweaty hair.

"It's okay," she said, "you're back, it's okay."

I trembled, resting my head on her shoulder as I breathed out tension in my chest. My muscles loosened as I melted against Elle's embrace, her hands reaching to hold her tight.

"I-I missed you s-so much," I stuttered.

"I missed you too," she whispered.

I smiled, warmth bursting within me as I squeezed her tighter. Yet my body locked up again once I glanced up, finding Eva and Louis standing in the centre of the room, staring down at the floor between them. In the middle of the room sat a single white candle and coil of rope curled around it like a snake protecting a treasure.

"You tried to kill me, didn't you?" she said, her voice light in disbelief.

"I—I had to," Louis replied.

His tone struck me. It was filled with a swelling desperation that took years away from him as he fell to his knees, gripping Eva's skirt as he gazed up at her with widened eyes. Eva began to sniffle, her hands cupping her face as she began to cry. Hearing it up close for the first time, the once-soft weeping had turned into frustrated sobs, each one filled with enough emotion to slice through whoever listened.

"I'm sorry, Eva," Louis said, his face muffled in her dress, "please don't be mad at me. I can make it better."

I felt Elle's hand clench around mine as Louis' eyes landed on us, his desperation melting away to reveal a determined sharpness, his jaw unlocked, like a wolf baring his teeth to a pair of cornered lambs.

"You want them to stay? You want your friends to stay?" he asked Eva, his breath hoarse, "I can make sure they stay."

He didn't wait for Eva's reply, rising to his feet to tower over her as his eyes remained locked on us. My gaze lowered to his hands, fingers flexed and ready to do what it had done so many times before, much like playing the keys on his piano.

"It's okay, you won't remember anything," he said, a slight grin across his face.

Elle and I lunged towards the door, panic bursting through me as the doorknob stiffened at my touch. I turned, reaching for my backpack, a scream falling from my mouth as a pair of hands latched onto my elbow, a foot tripping me as I was pulled to the ground. I coughed as the floor struck me, the backpack forced from my grip as Louis' hands wrapped around my throat, his weight pinning me to the floor.

This was real— I wasn't in a borrowed body. He was breathing in my ear, forcing the air from my lungs, trying to take what was mine. That smile came across his face again, his breathing turning into an animalistic growl as my head started to spin, my chest burning as it pleaded for oxygen.

"On second thought, maybe I won't kill you. You can remember everything, be aware of everything," he said between pants, "you'll be so out of your mind that you'll be begging me to kill you!"

I bent my neck forward, trying to catch one of his fingers between my teeth, my legs twisting beneath his knees as I tried to shove him off, my lungs straining for breath. Louis grinned, opening his mouth to release another laugh, only for his eyes to widen, his jaw tensing as a slight wheeze eased from his throat.

His grip on my throat loosened, his entire body stiffening as I glanced over his shoulder. Elle heaved as she hovered over him, her sweaty palms gripping the large kitchen knife that she'd sunk into the bend of his back. Her eyes, although filled with tears, held a burning fire. Her lips twisted into a violent snarl.

"You don't touch her!" she hissed.

Elle hauled her weight forward, forcing the blade down as Louis released a choking gasp. No blood oozed from the wound, the blade sparkling clean as it tore against his skin. His eyes grew, his jaw unlocked and gaping like a beached fish. My senses rushing back to me, I bent my knee, shoving it up into his stomach. The knife remained in his back as he tumbled sideways, a wheezing gasp easing from his mouth as his hands reached for the handle.

Elle's hands gripped my forearm, hauling me upwards. Her eyes filled with a burning fire, her face twisting into a snarl. She glanced back towards Eva, who stood with her back pressed against the wall and her hands clasped over her mouth.

"I am not one of your dolls!" Elle screamed.

Eva flinched before gradually bowing her head, a fresh trail of tears running down her cheeks. I turned back towards Louis as he began to pull the knife from his neck, wheezing with every inch of blade removed. I charged towards the door, gathering my backpack in one hand and Elle's forearm in the other. I wouldn't let her go— I wouldn't lose her again.

A plunging dread crashed over me as we reached the door. No matter how hard we slammed our bodies against it, it would not move. A low chuckle shot down the staircase, sending a prickling chill along my spine.

"You really are that stupid!" Louis snickered, the staircase creaking beneath his weight.

"Fuck!" I screamed, sweat dripping from my forehead, panic bursting inside me like firecrackers.

I latched onto the doorknob again, giving it a tug, then another, until it was open. I paused, surprise sticking me as the fresh air kissed my hot cheeks. I didn't question it, I just ran. I slowed my pace to ensure Elle stayed in my vision as we burst down the porch steps, her hair flowing behind her as she kept a grip on my hand, tears falling down her cheeks.

With a low cry, I flung my backpack ahead of us, watching as it tumbled through the iron gates. We followed, my heart bursting from my chest as I fell to my knees, grazing my hands against the rough ground. Elle collapsed beside me, her body trembling with every released breath. Rolling onto my back, I looked towards the house, my eyes narrowing to the figure by the gate.

The backpack laid at my feet, white powder oozing from the open pocket before lifting into the air like a gush of snow. Clifford watched with blank eyes, his body beginning to extend, his cheeks sinking and his jaw sharpening. Yet, as he grew older, his flesh began to rot further, the blackness of his eye sockets growing to consume the rest of his face and his teeth falling from his yellow gums.

Holding his breath, Clifford stepped forward and with a soft groan, his skin began to flake away, like white ash falling after a firestorm. As soon as his foot touched the outside of the gate, collapsed, falling forwards into a thin pile of ash before flowing away with the wind.

I was barely able to take in a breath before the front door swung open once again, my eyes fixating on both Mr. and Mrs.

Mortimer as they lunged from the house with Louis on their heels. He held the knife he'd pulled from his throat in his hand, waving it in the air as he charged after his parents.

"Get out! Both of you!" he barked.

Even from a distance, I could see their skin grow from a pale blue to a dull grey, rot and mold clinging to their skin and flesh, the years rushing back to them like debts paid. Their limbs could barely hold their bodies as they heaved like loose puppets, stumbling down the porch steps.

"You can't kick me out of my own house!" Mr. Mortimer barked, blood flowing from his mouth.

Louis flashed a smile, straightening his arm to point the blade at them, the hole in his throat gaping with every trembling breath.

"This is my house now!" he replied.

Mrs. Mortimer didn't hesitate, gripping the skirt of her dressing gown before sprinting towards the iron gate. Maybe she'd subconsciously learned not to underestimate her son. I gripped Elle's hand, scampering to the side of the gate. Mr. Mortimer followed after his wife, staggering as his hair faded to an ashy white.

"Wait, will you?" he barked.

"It's not my fault you can't keep up!" Mrs. Mortimer spat.

Like their trinkets, they shattered once they reached the gate, their moaning cries fading into the gentle breeze as they drifted away.

I finally let out a breath, falling back onto my elbows as relief crashed against me like a strong ocean wave. I watched as Louis dropped the knife to the grass, forgetting about us completely as he started to chuckle, growing into an uneven, chaotic fit of laughter. He bent over, bracing against his knees as he cackled.

"At last!" he screamed.

My eyes trailed up the house, my gaze locking onto a faint light in the second-story window. My eyebrows arched as I saw the newly-lit candle flickering against the dark, Eva's soft face floating like a mask behind it. My lips parted as the realisation hit me, a pile of questions following. Would he be mad at her? Could he do anything if he was? I glanced back down to Louis as he continued his celebration, shaking my head before lifting my gaze back up to Eva.

Eva lifted her hand, giving a small nod despite the tears glowing against her cheeks, mouthing a single word.

Go.

"Sorry about your backpack," Elle murmured.

"It's okay," I replied, readjusting my grip on her hand.

The darkness of the forest encased us as we passed through, the bitter cold of the night air seeping through our clothes. The trees still towered over us, regardless of time passed, we might as well have been the same little girls we'd been years before.

"Where can we go?" Elle asked.

The question slapped me like a hard backhand. I didn't know. I assumed we would go back 'home,' but I didn't really know where that was, the thought of returning to either of my parents' houses twisting my stomach. I doubt Elle felt any different, most likely worse.

I didn't know how long I'd been gone. I even attempted to check my watch before realising how stupid that idea was. The moment our feet touched the black top of the road, it felt odd— a discomforting familiarity. Elle's eyes danced around as we travelled what was once our normal route home, passing the first line of houses before reaching the shops. A lump formed in my throat as I noticed that the toy store was gone, switched with a news agency, and one of the restaurants had gone from Italian to a grill. The worry bubbled within me as we continued through the veil of the night. I felt a slight relief as I saw the phone booth still in its rightful place. I dug into my pocket to fish for change as Elle and I stepped inside, the streetlight pouring its blinding white rays down upon us.

"How long has this been here?" Elle asked.

"A while," I replied.

I reached into my pocket, pulling out the folded piece of paper within. I dialled the number, counting each drawn-out ring until finally a voice broke through.

"Yeah?"

I froze, a brief panic washing over me before I glanced at Elle. Snapping to my senses, I brought her hand to the phone, transferring it from my ear to hers. I listened to hear the blunt voice echo from the receiver.

"If this is a prank call, you can go fuck yourself," the voice spat.

Elle stuttered, releasing her grip from my hand before reaching to cradle the phone to her cheek.

"Jess?" she whispered.

"Elle?"

Elle's mouth hung open, her face blank before she finally choked out a response.

"Hey..." she said, her voice beginning to wobble, "it's really cold outside, can you come pick us up?"

The receiver crackled as the silence passed through. I held my breath before Jess finally whispered, "Yeah, um... where are you?"

With a long sigh, I slipped from the phonebooth, reversing as Elle leaned against the door, hunching her shoulders as if to cradle herself inwards. Letting the cold air caress my cheek, I slipped down to sit on the curb, resting my elbows on top of my knees. I noticed the tightness in my chest, reaching to press my hand against it, but it didn't soften. I felt a strange disappointment. I'd expected to maybe cry or need to take long, releasing breaths, but I didn't.

There are so many times when I'll feel that way again. Just sitting and soaking in my nothingness, waiting for something to come take me somewhere else.

Part Six

TIME INSIDE THE HOUSE PASSED like minutes, but I still felt the weight of the eighteen months I had been gone. It was as if the isolation all came rushing to me at once, being around 'normal' people setting off every nerve in my system. I felt lost in the noises that surrounded me, the distant chattering, the clicking of classroom doors and slamming of lockers. I narrowed my vision to the sliver of hallway in front of me, taking in what I could. I thought of retreating to the library before class, but I couldn't. I promised I'd wait for her.

I stood by the front office door, my hands in my pockets and my backpack digging into my shoulders. I stared down at my feet, watching the shadows of my fellow students passing me. I counted the types of shoes that passed me: runners, boots, flats, heels, until a pair of ankle boots stopped in front of me. I froze before my eyes travelled up towards the owner's face, my stomach flipping as I focused on their face.

"Hi."

Tina had grown a few extra inches, and her face was more angular. She'd added another earring to her collection. She'd changed her glasses to a pair of bright red frames and she'd cut her hair to just above her shoulders. I wanted to tell her how pretty she looked. I wanted to tell her that I missed her.

"I've been um, meaning to call, but I didn't want to intrude," she said, glancing down at her shoes.

"That's okay," I replied, "how are you?"

"Graduating soon, so, you know..."

She was like this when I first came back, sheepish and nervous as if I'd shatter if she said the wrong thing. That time was different though. I didn't realise why she was acting so strangely until a few years later, the thought striking me almost out of nowhere. She was scared of me. I mean, what kind of fifteen-year-old goes into the woods by herself, then comes back a year and a half later with her missing childhood friend? A child could have ignored the messed-up nature of that, but not someone who was almost an adult.

"Yeah... they put me back a few grades so I can catch up, so I don't know when I'll be graduating,"

"You're smart. I'm sure you'll be fine," she said.

Her voice was devoid in comparison to the enthusiastic pitch it had once held. I felt a prickling anxiety form within me just listening to it. My confusion left me the moment I recalled the reason I had not tried to reach out to her myself.

"Thanks," I said, taking a deep breath to prepare for my next sentence, "I'm sorry to hear about your dad."

I watched Tina's face, trying to find some flinching emotion, yet it remained still as she kept her eyes on the floor.

"If there's anything I can do to help, let me know," I said, almost desperate to get some kind of reaction from her.

"No, it's okay," she replied, her voice thin, "I'm just really glad you're back."

"Thanks," I replied.

She gave a light nod before turning away, slipping into the thin veil of the crowd. I watched her grow smaller with every step, keeping my eye on the back of her head until she disappeared around the corner. I felt my lips twist as I tried to hold back tears. I thought of what could've been, the amount of firsts I wanted to share with her. At the time, I couldn't imagine sharing them with anyone else and I thought she felt the same. I hadn't considered that she wouldn't wait for me.

I let out a sour sigh before leaning back to rest against the wall. I thought of running to the bathroom to release the tears that burned the back of my eyes, but I promised myself I wouldn't cry on my first day back. I was already the weird forest girl; I didn't want to be the crybaby either.

Like me, Elle stood out like a sore thumb thanks to the few gazes that followed her as she passed. She wore a heavy jumper and jeans, her hands resting on the straps of her backpack and her now waist-long hair into a thick braid that trailed behind her like a ball and chain. I lifted my hand to give a wave, snatching her from her daze.

"Hey," she murmured, sliding to stand next to me against the wall.

"How are you feeling?" I asked.

"It's a bit much," she replied, staring off into the ongoing crowd of students.

I gave her a nod before searching my mind for what to say next.

"What do you have first?" I asked.

Elle reached into her pocket to pull out her class schedule, unfolding it to scan her colour-coded timetable. She was placed three grades beneath her age in an attempt to catch her up. Although looking back on it, that would've put her apart from the students even more, as if being the 'weird missing girl' wasn't enough.

"English," Elle replied, "do you know where classroom 4b is?"

"Yeah, I have Biology in the same building," I replied, "follow me."

With that, I began to lead her down the hallway. Immediately, my thoughts fell back to the weeks before we stumbled into that house. Something as simple as walking through school was nothing to us, and to my dismay, I had gotten used to not having Elle beside me. I glanced over to her as she kept a firm grip on the straps of her backpack, her eyes darting around the corridor with each step we took.

I couldn't imagine what it was like for her. I had some time in between at least. She walked into that house a little girl and walked out a young woman with no preparation or guidance for what was expected of her. The remains of her childhood had been torn from her white, clenching knuckles.

Out of the corner of my eye, I spotted more gazes landing on us, followed by a few muffled whispers. They watched us as if two strange, misshapen birds had flown into the building—with a keen but cruel interest. One group wasn't subtle about it, gawking at us as we passed them. I felt the discomfort crawling over me like an unwanted touch. I frowned at them, raising my eyebrows and sharpening my gaze, but they didn't flinch. I swallowed my anger before leading Elle down a different corridor which would've taken us longer to get to our destination, but held less people.

I figured she would've noticed them, the urge to say something was itching my throat.

"Um, sorry about that," I said, "they're just idiots, just tell them to fuck off if they bother you."

Elle gave a slight nod, only seeming to take in a half of my sentence.

"What's going on in your head?" I asked.

Elle knitted her brows, her pace slowing as the hallway grew quiet. She took a long breath as I waited for her response.

"Even after everything... I'm not sure if I hate her," she said, "I thought I did, but... I don't know. I... it's not hate. I hate my parents, so I know what hate feels like. So, whatever it is, it's not hate."

"What do you mean?" I asked, confusion striking me, "she lured us in—she knew what she was doing."

"Yeah, but I don't think she wanted to hurt us. She wanted friends, someone other than...him to lean on," she mumbled, her voice growing quiet with every word, "but then again, she leaned too hard."

I turned to stare at the floor, my shoulders hunching under the weight of my backpack. My first thought was to hug her, and to this day, I wonder whether or not I should have. It just didn't feel right to me, like she wasn't ready for it. I instead reached to gently pat her shoulder, hoping that was enough.

I tried to focus on Elle and not my own racing thoughts, knowing they would poison me if I focused on them for too long. A part of me knew that I didn't hate Eva either, but I wasn't ready to accept that.

"That's not your fault," I said, "...so, she talked to you about stuff then?"

"Yeah," Elle replied, "after a while, I stopped replying though. I just was too tired. It was like she was draining me, but she'd just stare off into the corner and talk. I don't think anyone had ever listened to her."

I hummed, staring off to the side.

"She kinda reminded me of you sometimes," I said.

I don't know why I said that. It just slipped from my mouth, leaving room for a sudden regret.

"Er, sorry, not in a bad way," I said.

Elle tilted her head, a dark dreaminess filling her eyes as a light, yet bitter smile spread across her face.

"Funny... I was going to say the same thing about you."

Her response struck me hard, my arms pressing against my ribs as I felt a slight spark of anger within me. Yet, I couldn't deny it.

"Fair," I murmured, "...but you miss her, don't you?"

I didn't look at Elle to see her reaction, keeping my eyes forward as I guided her. We kept our silence, stewing in our individual emotions before I parked us beside the classroom door.

"This is it," I said, glancing down before choking out a meek, "I guess I'll see you later."

I gave her an awkward smile before stepping away, turning to face the long hallway.

"Zoe."

I stopped in my tracks, somewhat relieved as I twisted around to face her. My stance loosened as I noticed how her hands gripped her books, her spine arched and her shoulders hunched as she gazed at the ground.

"...I never said thank you for those apple slices," she said.

I frowned before the memory came back to me, leaving me at a loss before I stuttered out—

"Oh, i-it's okay, no big deal."

"No, it was," she insisted, her voice falling bluntly.

Silence came between us once again. I couldn't find the words with which to reply, leaving me to simply gawk at her. She lifted her eyes to meet mine before stepping back, reaching for the classroom door, then slipping inside. I remained in the hallway, unmoving as several students passed me, rushing upon the call of the bell.

I stood there, tears brimming behind the lenses of my eyes. I still can't pinpoint what I was crying about, just that it felt like both a reviving breath and a knife to my chest all at once.

We didn't speak much after that. There was so much to talk about, but we had nothing to say. I felt somewhat disappointed, as if I was owed something from it all, at the very least a best friend. Yet, it wasn't going to happen. We couldn't stay the same, we couldn't stay children forever.

Yet, like she was over those years she was gone, Elle was still there. She exists in the back of my mind, clinging to my thoughts, sometimes taking up the whole space for herself.

A few years later, she would drive me to my father's house after I came out to my mother. I helped her move out of her parents' house when she was sixteen. They had screamed after her, desperate to regain their rock they'd grown so used to leaning on. She went to live with Jess in the big city, coming back only for school. Then we graduated.

We check in on each other often, sending each other birthday cards and gifts during the holiday season. We chat on the phone sometimes, or via Zoom, although I prefer a phone call because I hate seeing the wrinkles that have started to crawl across her face. She asks about Sara and the cafe we own together, and then tells me about her PhD and her nephews. The last time I saw her in person was at Jess' funeral.

Every time I see or hear from her, I have the urge to ask or to talk about it. I never do. Someday I might, if I find the words.

I still have dreams of those corridors, my tiny feet carrying me through the thick shadows. Their voices creep into my head, bouncing around until they pull me from sleep. I normally don't wake Sara, but if I do, she'll hold me, lulling me back to sleep to the soft sound of her voice.

We occasionally have people show up at our house, documentary people or journalists wanting to know why two little girls went into a forest and simply disappeared for years at a time. One time, Sara chased a top psychological researcher off our front lawn with a broom after I said 'no' to participating in his stupid study. I called Elle later that day to warn her to look out for him.

I feel bad knowing I haven't told Sara the truth, or at least, the truth I know. Yet, I know she understands and I know she loves me.

One day, after months of ignoring the intrusive thought, I decided to go back. Elle didn't know what to say about the idea, just 'be careful.' I drove for the first couple of hours before letting Sara take the wheel, allowing me to watch as the pine trees began to surround us.

She was somewhat giddy about the experience, having never seen my hometown before, but she kept the questions to a minimum, knowing our true destination. The first wave of dread came over me once we reached the outer layer of houses. I forced myself to remain silent as we passed my childhood home, yet my eyes were glued to it as we passed by. Sara opened her mouth to ask, but said nothing. Then came the centre of town, the phone booth, the school, before I told Sara to pull over.

She parked in the hairline of the forest, my shoes slapping against the road as I stepped from the car. Sara followed, dressed in a thick beige jumper with her hair dyed a reddish brown to cover up the grey streaks that had begun to sprout from her head. Her face was covered in freckles, her smile causing these cute dimples in her cheeks. She wore her signature red lipstick that made her known to regulars at our café, and the olive-green apron she wears when she's making the fresh scones and 'muffin of the day.'

"Shit, Z," Sara said, pressing the driver's side door closed, "you used to play out here? I would've died for this much space as a kid."

I laughed, a slight smile gracing my face as I rounded the car to meet her.

"City girl," I mocked.

Sara grinned at me before taking my hand, rubbing her thumb against my knuckle before staring off into the woods.

"If you want to turn back, we can," she said, "it's okay if you don't want to go."

I parted my lips, a long-held hesitation swelling within me as I gazed into the curtains of trees, the eerie silence consuming me as I took in a slow breath. I stepped forward with Sara at my side. The moment my foot met the dirt, I felt it again. The slight murmur that pulled me in the right direction through the trees, gradually building into a soft, toxic lullaby. A lump swelled in my throat, the soft autumn breeze prickling my skin as we continued through the woods. Sara just held my hand, giving it a light squeeze every once and while in an attempt to ground me. It mostly worked, but my mind kept wandering, wrapped in the siren's song whilst envisioning the memories locked in the damp forest.

My chest started to twist as the ground began to incline slightly, rising until I saw it, peeking out from out from the trees like a rat I thought I'd poisoned long ago. There were still deep track marks in the dirt from when they'd tried to tear it down. Yet, even the crew's largest machines couldn't do it. They had apparently entered the house, only to find it as torn and old as the outside. I guess Eva didn't want to play with them.

I felt Sara give my hand a comforting squeeze, her way of silently asking if I was okay. I didn't respond, raking my vision up the house until I reached that tower, gazing into the crumbling window. Then it came, the song. It was soft in my ear, yet the tug was strong and all too familiar. With the song, she followed, appearing in the window, remaining not a day older from when I last saw her.

She stopped singing, blinking down at me before giving me a light wave. I'm surprised she recognised me with greys in my hair and wrinkles carved into my face.

"Can we go home now?" Sara asked, "I'm sorry— I just don't like this place. It feels just...bad."

I glanced back up towards the house, my muscles tensing as he stepped into view, placing his hands firmly against Eva's shoulders as he peered down at me. Thinking back on it, I still can't translate his gaze. His eyes squinted, yet his expression was soft with one eyebrow slightly perked, as if he was somewhat irritated, perhaps? He seemed to humph before stepping from the window, taking Eva with him.

"You go on ahead," I told Sara, "just give me another minute."

Sara nodded, reaching to rub her forehead before starting to wander back down the trail. I glanced over my shoulder, watching her shrink with every step before turning back towards the house. I eyed the door, tucking my hands into my pockets as it nudged open. I held my breath as Eva slid her foot out, edging onto the porch before softly closing the door behind her. She glanced down the steps as if she were descending a mountain, climbing down before making her way across the porch. She held her arms across her chest, pressing a book against her gown before she met me just in front of the gate.

"Hello."

Her glistening eyes fell downwards as she teased the ground with her heels. I'd thought about what to say the whole drive there, yet it all washed away in an instant.

"Why are you here?" she asked.

I clicked my tongue, toying with my answer in my head.

"Closure, I guess," I muttered, "or maybe I want to stop being so mad at you. I'm tired of it."

Eva lowered her eyes once again, lifting the book from her chest with the cover facing her. It was ratted and aged, the edges worn with the pages beginning to fall from the spine.

"I read it over and over again," she said, running her palm across the cover.

She lifted her eyes, glancing past me into the woods, her throat wobbling as she swallowed.

"Are there trolls out there?" she asked.

"Yeah, sometimes," I sighed.

Eva stared down at the grass, seeming to fall into a numbing daze before she took in a long, sharp breath. She reached into the pocket of her dress, pulling out the candlestick with the harmless flame stick flickering.

"I'm sorry for what I did to you, and to Elle. It was wrong," she said, holding the candle out towards me, "can you help me, please?"

My eyes fell to the candle, forever glowing with light, unable to be put out or melted away. The cogs in my brain turned, contrasting thoughts flying around my head like bees around a hive. I looked into Eva's whitened eyes, searching for any hints of deception. I saw my reflection in them, squinting down with a stern frown. Eva waited patiently, her hand still firmly clutching the candle until I finally replied.

"I can help, but you have to do the rest yourself," I said, "and you have to promise me that you're not playing me. If I sense that you are, I'm out of here."

Eva blinked at me, fear rushing through her panicked eyes as she brought the candle closer to her chest. I don't know if she expected me to turn her down.

"And I'm not doing this because you unlocked the door for us, that doesn't make up for it," I said, "I'm doing this because I want to."

She gave me a light nod before taking a step back, bending down to rest the candle on the grass beneath her. She backtracked some more, squeezing the book into a hug before glancing at me expectantly. I looked back up at the house, hesitance filling my stomach.

"Where is he?" I asked.

"I don't know," she replied.

I took in a long breath, keeping it in my lungs as I kept my eyes on Eva. Biting back any hesitance, I took a step towards her, teasing the threshold of the gates. I paused, as if giving her a final warning before taking another step. I flinched as I felt the breeze halt, the air murky and old. I didn't take my eyes off of Eva, watching as silent tears trickled from her eyes as I bent down to pick up the candle.

I gave her another long stare. I think I was waiting for her to stop me, but she didn't, she just let another tear fall before I stepped back, the wax crumbling into a thin, red ash as I did so.

Eva gasped, the book falling from her grasp as her spine began to extend, her waist widening and limbs extending as she grew. She began to reflect the life she should have lived, her skin tanning as if she'd spent hours in the sun and fine lines forming around her mouth from years she could've spent smiling.

"Eva!"

My eyes shot towards the front door as it flung open, smacking the wall with a loud crack. Louis emerged from the house. His eyes were wide with panic, burning with rage.

"Come inside! What are you doing? I can't protect you out there!" he barked, rushing down the stairs.

Eva didn't look back at him, black tears rolling down her cheeks as wrinkles began to line her eyes and forehead. With a wheezing breath, she lunged forward. I stepped back as she burst, white ash falling from her lips and bursting through her eye sockets before sweeping up into the breeze that carried her away like a hoard of cloud-coloured moths.

I watched as Eva faded into the sky, moulding into the clouds before I turned back around. Louis stood in the centre of the yard, his jaw slack and his eyes gawking at the space his sister had once taken up. His shoulders sunk and he lowered his gaze to the ground, maintaining a cold silence. He didn't say anything to me, or do anything at all. He turned, his arms dangling by his sides as if he'd forgotten how to use them before he wandered back to the house, floating up the porch stairs, before disappearing behind the door.

After the click of the door, I let out a long breath, a tear rolling down my cheek as a wave of rage rushed through me. I glanced back up at the house, still standing strong despite its crumbling appearance. As long as the house had him, it would remain standing like a black shadow burned into the back of my head.

I met Sara at the bottom of the hill, her hand finding herself as she gave me a weak smile.

"Sorry if I freaked you out," she said, "I just felt really weird all of a sudden."

"That's okay," I replied, "sorry, I should've just come by myself."

Sara's eyebrows dented before she stepped forward, pressing a soft kiss against my lips. The usual explosion of heat rushed through me, a blush blooming on my cheeks. Sara smiled at that, wrapping her arms around me, her warmth smothering some of the cold that had grown within me.

"You're not alone, beautiful," she whispered.

She looped her arm over my shoulder as we began to dip back into the forest, yet my mind remained on the house. I felt a sudden swelling in my chest as I came to the realisation that that's where a part of me, whether I liked it or not, would remain. Regardless of how both Elle and I had grown, we were still two lost little girls in that house. We're still in there, huddling in corners and running down halls, and we're never coming home. I know I have Sara, I have my friends and chosen family, I even have Elle sometimes. But at times, when I'm locked in my own mind, I feel as if I am nothing but the shell that remains.

Acknowledgements

I'm so grateful for the wonderful Stephanie Sanders-Jacob for picking up this book and putting so much hard work and talent into perfecting it. Also, to David-Jack Fletcher of Slashic Horror Press for passing the manuscript on to its now-home at Squirm Books.

As always, endless thanks to Loretta, my found sister and bestest best friend. Thank you for always believing in me, supporting my writing and for always making me a pot of peppermint tea when I need it most.

And thank to Briana, Sarah, Mini and Annie for being the best friends a gay, neurodivergent girl could ask for.

About the Author

C laire L. Smith (she/her) is an Australian author, graphic designer and visual artist.

Her debut gothic horror novella, 'Helena' was published by CLASH Books and her most recent novel, 'Agnes and Cat' is a body/folk horror story inspired by fae folklore. Her short story 'The Last Runt' was a part of the Ditmar Award-Nominated horror collection 'This Fresh Hell' by Clan Destine Press.

She has illustrated and designed covers for a range of presses and publications including Ghost Orchid Press, Cemetery Gates Media, The Ghastling Press, Tenebrous Press and more.